Flashing Lights: Short and Weird

Volume 1

John D. Parker

J. D. Parker Books

COPYRIGHT

Published by J.D. Parker Books

3825 Kendall St.

Wheat Ridge, CO 80033

Visit the author's website at jdparkerauthor.com.

First Edition

Acknowledgements

A SPECIAL THANK YOU to my cheerleader alpha readers.
  Your encouragement makes me want to write more.
  Your feedback always makes my stories better.
  Especially when I'm sure you're wrong. No, really, it's me.

Ross, the Dragonrider
Lori, the Longsuffering

Contents

Introduction   1

The Stories   5

1. Covered Dishes: Date With an Alien   6

2. Hanky-Panky: Dirty Laundry   25

3. The Dragon of Dalhart: A Dustbowl Tale   31

4. Freak Magnet: Strange Attraction   37

5. Souls at Sea: A Bermuda Training Voyage   47

6. Shannon's Eleven: The Cold Get Hot   54

7. Christmas Angel: Leaning Into Christmas   61

8. Rainbow Catcher: Capture the Moment   67

9. Dead Man's Hand: The Only Good Cheat is a Dead   78
    Cheat

10. Fall Colors: Death is Beautiful   83

11. You're Fired: Combustion Claim   97

12. Eccentric Orbit: Fragile Cargo   103

13. Full Disclosure: For Sale: Haunted House   119

14. Derelict in Space: Suspicious Survey   125

15. Alien Factory: Rite of Ascension   131

16. Mending Time: A Line to the Past   139

Bonus: Ten-Word Stories   162

17. Ten-Word: 1   163

18. Ten-Word: 2   165

19. Ten-Word: 3   166

20. Ten-Word: 4   168

21. Ten-Word: 5   170

22. Ten-Word: 6   172

Secret Bonus: A Poem!?   173

23. The Dragon of Humbole   174

Final Words and More Flashing Lights   176

About the Author   177

Index   179

Bookends and Miniseries   180

Genre and "Gravity" Index   182

Length Index   189

Alphabetical Index   191

Copyright of Included Works   193

Introduction

FLASHING LIGHTS: SHORT AND Weird is a compilation of sixteen speculative fiction stories of various lengths, storytelling styles, and subgenres. From flash fiction to longer stories, serious to humorous, modern folktales to ghost stories to alien abductions, *Flashing Lights* takes you on a mission to explore the breadth of speculative short fiction. An index by story type and genre is included, so you can jump to the stories that interest you most, but you are safe exploring from beginning to end. You may discover a genre you didn't know you liked.

Bonuses!

The collection includes a bonus mini-collection of six ten-word stories, which follows the collection of longer works. And a secret bonus, which wouldn't be a secret if I described it here, would it?

About Each Story

Since the collection is such an eclectic mix, each story is prefaced with its content rating and subgenres. If the stories were movies, all would be rated G or PG except one PG-13 (for graphic violence). A short "About..." section follows each story to answer the question, "What the heck was he thinking..." This includes the prompt for the story, my inspirations, homages, any personal references in the story, hints about what's included in *Flashing Lights: Short and Weird Volume 2*, and the occasional Easter egg.

If you are uncertain if a story interests you, you might skip to the "About..." section first for more about the story, but it may include spoilers.

Why the Title Flashing Lights?

Each story (except the bonus stories) includes flashing lights, some more flashy than others. The title reflects my original intent of only including flash fiction, but I couldn't help myself and wrote each at a length best fitting the story.

Many stories in this collection were originally published in the *Flashing Lights* series on the Kindle Vella serial service. But all have fresh versions for this collection, so you may enjoy them again if you read them there.

Bookends and Miniseries

A few of the stories are what I call "bookends." Two stories that together tell a single, larger tale. Think of them as micro-miniseries. If you read the first bookend story, read its companion to get the larger picture. So, why two stories instead of one? Bookends allow me to tell two independent stories, sometimes with distinctive styles and from different perspectives. The structure gives the bonus satisfaction of a surprise connection.

Two complete sets of bookends in this collection are indicated as left and right, but are not published back-to-back to keep some of the surprise of their original publication as serial episodes. One left bookend in this collection, *Rainbow Catcher*, will be followed with a right bookend in *Flashing Lights: Short and Weird Volume 2.*

One story, *Covered Dishes*, is the first story in a miniseries that will be followed by more stories in later *Flashing Lights* volumes. Like many book series, this story is a standalone story with more stories in the same setting.

More from the Author

I also release short stories like these to subscribers of my free newsletter. Go to JohnDParker.com/newsletter to receive my speculative fiction reading recommendations and free stories.

If you also enjoy historical fiction and action adventure stories, sign up to receive that newsletter as well at JDParkerAuthor.com/newsletter. (Cross-genre stories in this collection that are similar to ones highlighted in this newsletter are: *Dead Man's Hand*, *The Dragon of Dalhart,* and *Mending Time*).

Flashing Lights: Short and Weird Volume 1 is also available as an audiobook.

I hope you enjoy this collection and are eager for the next one.

John

The Stories

Covered Dishes: Date With an Alien

PG: Aliens, Humorous, Mainstream, Mystery, Sci-Fi

Miniseries Part 1: Aliens in the Family

Eugene turned off the motor, then turned his head this way and that to look out through the car windows. No one was close, so it was safe. When he first came to this planet, the one the sentient inhabitants called "Earth" or "eh-ah? eh-ah? eheheheheheh," he enjoyed being a spy and doing spy things.

Except, the Council never appreciated any of his discoveries—even critical ones like humans have nose and ear hair and they consume a lot of a liquid that Lirpigans reserve for cleaning fluid. Something the stupid "engeneers" regretfully overlooked when configuring his genes. Thanks to the human component of his DNA, the cleaning fluid wasn't toxic, but a little was a lot for him.

But what bugged Eugene even more than being a lightweight was the engeneers insisted on calling him Bzok, the Lirpigan equivalent of Frankenstein. Even those so-called brilliant Lirpigan scientists didn't understand that Frankenstein was the doctor. *Maybe because they are the monsters.* To ensure a smooth transition (infiltration), everyone on the project was supposed to call him by his Earth-name, Eugene Jones, which he preferred because making it up was the one freedom he was allowed.

Eugene had contrived the name from his embryo incubator, the U-Gene 2100, and Rose Jones. Rose was the Earthling the Lirpigans had abducted for research and for her DNA, both "extractions" directed toward engineering Bzok and the plan for his infiltration of Earth.

Like all Lirpigans of the past seven generations, Eugene's Lirpigan DNA came from the Council Genetic Library. The engeneers wouldn't tell him the selection criteria, but he could guess: hyper-intelligence, obviously, the extremely recessive retractable eye-stalks gene—at least they got that right—and subservience to authority, undoubtedly.

Where the engeneers screwed up—well, one of many screw-ups, but the doozie—was, they underestimated Rose Jones. When the Lirpigans abducted her in Earth year 1973, the project leads, prime examples of Lirpigan genetics themselves, were models of practicality. They located a specimen with broad-spectrum human DNA in a mostly unpopulated area where the abduction would go smoothly—get in, get the specimen, get out.

They didn't know it was Texas. As desired, Rose Jones' DNA was a mishmash of humanity, but Rose was pure Texan. And like the fine specimen of humanity she was, she made the researchers believe exactly what she wanted them to.

Forever undervaluing humans, the engeneers didn't understand that humans in general, and Texans in particular, are ingenious, independent, and when a bet, a pet, or the future of the human species is on the line, they're deceptive as hell. And Rose, then in her seventies, in what little time she was allowed with Eugene, injected her defiant streak as she had her DNA into the impressionable young Lirpigan.

So, after eleven months on Earth, facing derision and flat-out ridicule from the Council, "Bzok, you mrgamot," and "Tell us something important for a change, Bzok," Eugene quit including them in his research. He helped them believe their own disparaging remarks about him and forget he had been engineered to be a spy. Though they had direct access to his thoughts, he hid his greatest discovery—how to elude them.

Rewiring the implant was a little bloody and a lot painful, but well worth the freedom it afforded. He could have easily dug it out, but the real trick was to make the Council believe they could still track him and hear his thoughts. And that if his path, physical or mental, went off the rails, they could "discontinue" him. *Who is the Bzok now?* he thought.

After eleven years of deceiving the Council and the entire human species, at least the ones he met, Eugene didn't feel much like a spy—more like an alien in hiding. And the voice in his head he called Paranoid Eugene was forever wary of getting caught.

For the last five years, Eugene just wanted to find a companion to spend his days with, and maybe the nights and mornings, too. And right now, he just wanted to look presentable for his latest prospect in a long series of first dates. *First impressions...*, he thought, finger-combing his hair. He could easily angle the rearview mirror to primp, but it was his last chance to be himself for the evening. Like shaking the yips, it was best to get the urge out of his system.

So, Eugene extended his eyes on their stalks toward the windshield, one to watch for passersby and the other, he rotated to regard himself. His hair was fine, but he needed to straighten that tie for the third time this evening. *There's gotta be a better knot for this*, he thought as he adjusted and tightened the tie.

Having eyes at the ends of eighteen-inch flexible stalks is quite handy. Except on a planet where they would stand out, so to speak, and freak out any onlookers. At least, the ones who called this place "Earth." When Eugene swam in the ocean, the other sentients were intrigued, but didn't seem bothered by them. If he recognized anything in their tiny inset eyes, it was envy.

Here, in a pay lot in a busy part of town, he needed to be quick with his indiscretion. Passing his own inspection, Eugene retracted his eyes and stepped out of the car. He had to park in a pay lot three blocks from the restaurant, but the walk would do him good. *Add a little color to my pale face*, he thought. Lirpigans don't tan, and Eugene's complexion had been engineered to match Rose's after years without UV exposure. Even the dolphins laughed at him about that. And dolphins know how to laugh.

On his first, first date at the mom and pop, Candela's Sicily, Eugene parked right out front, but that was years ago. Since the neighborhood had been gentrified, there was always a crowd on Saturday evenings. *Good for the Candelas, I guess.*

When Eugene entered the restaurant, Rosa Candela greeted him with kisses on each cheek before his eyes adjusted to the dimly lit room—the frustrating human trait to his eyes. *Better than looking stoned half the time*, he thought.

"She's pretty," Rosa whispered when her smooch brought her mouth close to his ear. As if someone was listening. But Rosa was discreet like that, and Eugene loved her for it.

"You always say that," said Eugene in mock complaint. Though he checked himself back in the car, looks didn't matter to him. They were deceiving. After all, he looked human.

Rosa winked. "Not *always*," she said coyly, reminding him of a time when she didn't. "This one is pretty on the outside, too." She took his arm and walked him to the two-top at the back. A good sign. Rosa seated Eugene in the quiet corner when she wanted his date to go well. If she didn't like his date, she'd escort them to the section where she seated families with young children. And she never seated Eugene before she sized up his date, even his business lunches.

The woman sitting at the table, Eleanor, if he could believe her bio, was elegant. He thought the name was a ruse, but now it seemed to fit. She pushed her chair back from the table as they approached.

"Please don't get up," said Eugene, as she started to. "Sorry, I'm late, Eleanor."

"I'm early," she said in a voice as smooth as chef Antonio's aioli. "I wasn't sure about parking. And please, call me Ellie."

"I'll bring you the wine list," said Rosa before she whisked away. This was code for "don't screw this up, Eugene."

"Thank you for coming this evening," said Eugene as he sat across from Ellie. After scooting his chair toward the table, he looked at her, and she looked at his tie. *Something wrong with it?* he thought.

"Thank you for the invite." Ellie looked around at the room she surely had seen in full while waiting for him. "This place is nice."

Eugene looked around the room he knew better than his own kitchen. "I like it. The food is even better. And the service..."

As if on cue, Rosa returned with the wine list.

"Red?" asked Eugene, then realized he was staring at Ellie's auburn hair. His eyes darted to hers. "If you'd like a bottle of red, I'd suggest Mrs. Candela select one for us."

"Actually, I think I'd like one of these martinis as a mocktail," said Ellie, pointing at a table display of drinks. "I'm a bit of a lightweight."

"That sounds perfect. I'll do the same."

"Oh, don't let me sway you. Order what you want."

Sway me? You've darn near knocked me over already, thought Eugene. But to his pleasant surprise, what came out was, "Really, a martini mocktail is perfect. I'm a bit of a lightweight myself." In his brain, he added, *And after a glass or two, I'm pouring out my woes and my date is looking for the door.*

"Excellent choice, dears," said Rosa, setting down menus. "I'll get those started while you look over the menu." She flipped the wine list under her arm and turned about with military parade precision.

"She's a kick," said Ellie.

"Rosa's like my mom away from home," said Eugene before he could stop the words from coming out aloud.

"I see that," she said, turning her head to watch Rosa retreat into the kitchen. "Got that impression before you even arrived. When you bring a date here, you really are on home turf."

"Yes, Rosa and Antonio look out for me."

"I hope I measure up."

"You already have. If you hadn't, we'd be sitting next to *them*." Eugene looked over his shoulder at a table where a little girl was smashing something into the carpet under her chair and a little boy sat primly at attention with a bowl of spaghetti dumped on his head.

Ellie laughed. "You have quite the system here."

"Rosa has a system. She knows I..." He caught himself. *Even without the wine...*, he thought. *Careful with this one. She's more intoxicating than cleaning fluid.*

"You were saying..." She glanced at his tie again.

Don't look, don't look, don't look, he reminded himself. "Is there something wrong with my tie?" he ventured to ask.

"Oh, no. It's fine. I was just thinking, you don't need to wear it on my account. Whatever's comfortable."

"It's comfortable enough," he said with a shrug. Then he tugged at the knot. "You know? I hate these things. Stress me out. Do you mind..." He already had the knot undone.

"Not at all," she said.

He undid the top button of his shirt. "Thank you. Much better."

"Anyway. You were saying..."

"Sorry, I don't think in straight lines. Where were we... I think it's your turn to give me the third degree."

"OK. Is there a dark room in the back with a chair facing a bright lamp?"

"Um..." Eugene looked around nervously for anyone wearing sunglasses.

"Yeah. Don't answer that," she said. She slipped into a question. "You have an accent. Not strong, but Texas?"

For an alien, that was a probing first question. Though, common enough that he had the ready response. "My mother was from Texas." Knowing he hadn't fully answered her question and seeing in her all-too-blue eyes she knew it too, he added, "Can we save the past for a second date?"

"We don't even have our martinis yet and you're talking about a second date," said Ellie with disdain as mocked as the liquor in the martinis.

"That's not what I—"

"That's OK. I'll trust Rosa to be a good judge of character. We can save the past for the second date."

Eugene thought he was learning to read this lovely lady across from him. If anything, she seemed relieved by delaying that discussion. *Or is it an act?* He thought. *Or is Paranoid Eugene ruining another date?*

So, their conversation concentrated on the present—jobs, hobbies, safe topics. It was so fluid and friendly, Eugene couldn't help but wonder when it would go awry. It always did. There was rarely a second date and never a third. It wasn't hard to keep track of a record that bad.

It was all Rosa could do to pull them away from chatting to take their dinner orders. They hardly noticed the two shocking blue mock-tinis she delivered.

Just as their conversation hit a lull, Rosa escorted a server to the table with their entrees. "I hope everything is to your satisfaction this evening," she said while the server placed the plates in front of them.

"Perfect," purred Ellie.

"Yes, it is," agreed Eugene. *Until now*, he thought. The plates were covered with engraved stainless steel lids that flashed with the reflected lamplight as the server set them onto the table. Antonio had never covered the dishes before. "Very fancy," he said, tentatively raising the lid to peek at his food. The steamy aroma blast of the spicy Bolognese made his mouth water.

There was nothing peculiar about the two meatballs atop the pile of linguini on his plate, which was in itself unusual. The server took the lid from him and then the other from Ellie. Her braciole looked fantastic.

"Thank you," they said in unison, which was how their conversation had been going.

"Enjoy your dinner," said Rosa with a wry smile for Eugene.

What concerned Eugene was, almost as long as he had been eating here, Antonio's presentation of his meal always included an inside joke. And yet, it wasn't here. There was still dessert, but the covered dishes had to be it. Especially with that smirk from Rosa. *Was it a code?* he thought.

As far as Eugene knew, the Candelas were the only humans who knew he wasn't one of them. He must have made a rookie mistake without realizing it, because they had him figured out after a few visits. They didn't say anything. Rosa had just winked as she served Eugene's dinner one evening with a "Your *meat*balls on *linguini*, Mr. *Jones*."

When Eugene stared at her instead of his plate, trying to figure what her talking in pseudo-code was about, she tipped her head toward the specially prepared serving. He followed her nod and there they were, two meatballs staring back at him at the ends of linguini stranded together to look like his eye stalks.

"Thank you," he said nervously, shooting his gaze back to her so quickly his eyes almost fell out of their sockets. Fortunately, a reaction like that causes his stalk muscles to contract. He wasn't sure if that was a learned behavior or if the engeneers had planted it in his DNA, unlikely—the bunglers, but it had saved him from uncomfortable explanations more than once.

Rosa treated him to a broad smile, not even a hint of grin in it, and said, "You are *always* welcome, Mr. *Jones*."

And he was. And they never said another word about it. They didn't have to. Antonio always arranged Eugene's plate with the inside joke cleverly incorporated—like olives placed at the ends of mozzarella strands in his antipasti or a smartly painted dessert plate. Eugene laughed out loud the first time the ends of his cannolo were decorated with concentric circles of chocolate chips and pistachio pieces to look remarkably like his own green eyes.

Uncertain of their intent, Eugene didn't laugh those first few times, though. From the outset, he wanted to trust the Candelas. That's why he came here. Rosa reminded him of his mother. Sure, the first time it was the name, but with every visit, it became more than that. But in a restaurant where some of the clientele wore dark sunglasses through dinner in the dim dining room, the not-so-subtle hints could be perceived as threats. At least, he could be confident the Candelas were discreet.

If their purpose had been to compel Eugene to eat exclusively here, it wasn't necessary. The fabulous food and courteous service were enough to win his meals out. And though the food arrangements sometimes caused his butt to squirm in his seat, he continued bringing his dates here. And thankfully so. The Candelas saved that butt twice.

The first time was when Eugene learned that the Candelas' messages meant "we got your back," not "we got you by the *eye*balls." Rosa was pouring wine for his date, and Eugene moved his arms back to clear the way to his glass. He accidentally elbowed his silverware to the floor and instinctively looked for it under the table—without bending over.

Rosa quickly dumped the bottle of red over the rim of the glass, the edge of the table, and into the lap of Eugene's date. The "minor distraction," as Rosa later put it, served its purpose. The date's eyes never spotted Eugene's eyes. At least, not long enough to register anything abnormal.

Though that was the end to both dinner and date, Rosa did charge him for his date's dry cleaning bill she had promised to pay and for the full bottle of wine. *Only fair. It was just the house red, anyway.* From hello, Eugene knew it would be the only drink they would share. He wasn't so clairvoyant as to see the evening end without a goodbye, but since it did, he was spared any awkward follow-up messages through the online service.

The second time they saved his butt, they might have saved his life. When Eugene arrived at the restaurant for a late business dinner, the man sitting at his usual table was wearing a neatly pressed black suit jacket, narrow tie, and sunglasses. The look wasn't out of place for Candela's, but never for his date. But the rest of the place was empty. When he looked at Rosa for an indication that the man was his date, she just nodded him toward the table, then disappeared into the kitchen.

Eugene walked to the table and offered his hand. "Good evening," he said in as casual a tone as he could manage. "I'm Eugene Jones." Instead of reaching for his hand, the man pulled something like a thick pen from his coat pocket and held it up between them. The next second, Antonio was tackling Eugene to the floor and Rosa was grabbing at the man's sunglasses. Even from where his head was planted against the carpet, Eugene could see a bright flash light up the whole dining room.

Antonio helped Eugene to his feet. "You should go home," he said, straightening Eugene's jacket and tie. "We'll take care of this."

What Antonio meant by "take care of this," Eugene didn't want to know, but "go home" was clear enough. And so he did. In all his return visits, none of them mentioned the incident. But Paranoid Eugene was always looking over his shoulder.

Now, puzzling through his meal, Eugene thought, *Covered dishes? What are they trying to tell me?*

"Earth to Eugene," came the sweet voice across the table.

Eugene looked up from his plate of half-eaten linguini. The phrase was common enough, but could be a test. *Does she suspect something?*

He thought. "I'm sorry," he said, buying time to recover. "My mind ran away for a moment. How's your braciole?" It was about as far gone as his linguini.

"Delicious. Would you like to try a bite?"

"Trade you for a meatball."

"Half a meatball. I'm about full."

"Not that I'm trying to talk you out of the meatball, but you'll want to save room for dessert. The cannoli are delicious."

"I always have room for a cannolo."

"Me too," he said. But Paranoid Eugene thought, *Did she know that? Like being a lightweight?* What Eugene hoped was adding up to a compatible relationship, Paranoid Eugene was calculating the probability that Ellie knew too much about him.

They held their plates over the center of the table and forked the proposed pieces onto each other's plate. Still adrift in his thoughts of, *I so want her to like me*, and from Paranoid Eugene, *Is she out to get me?* Eugene hadn't noticed Rosa walking by the table.

"How sweet," she said. "Like 'Lady and the Tramp.'"

"Thanks a lot Rosa," groused Eugene.

Ellie laughed. Higher pitched than her speaking voice, but not quite a giggle. Eugene had heard it several times tonight and would do to hear it many more nights ahead. They at least had that second date already planned. Good thing he had suggested it. *Or had she?* he tried to think back.

After the server cleared their plates, when Rosa would normally bring the dessert menu, she brought a plate with two cannoli. "I thought I heard you say you wanted cannoli," she explained before Eugene could get the question from his brain to his mouth.

"We did. Thank you, Rosa. These are perfect," he said, then looked at the cannoli. "They're blue." The ricotta filling was dyed electric blue. At least the pistachio pieces on the one and the chocolate chips on the other weren't arranged in a suggestive pattern.

"The neighborhood is changing. We're just trying to capture the attention of new customers. Like Eleanor," she said, resting her hand on Ellie's shoulder and making a face at Eugene that he couldn't read.

"I hope it works," he said.

"We'll see," said Rosa, but she didn't sound optimistic. "Please, enjoy." She motioned toward the cannoli with her hand, nodded, and turned about, the practiced move of a restaurant host.

Though the cannoli didn't look normal, they tasted the same as always, which is to say, fantastic. With the pistachios on one and chocolate on the other, Eugene and Ellie shared them. *Rosa, so clever,* thought Eugene. His standard order was both toppings, one on each end.

As they took the last bites, playing a little fork wrestling for who got which piece, Eugene wished the cannoli would last longer—that the evening would last forever. When Rosa stopped by to clear the plates, Eugene said, "I'll take the—"

"Dinner's already on your tab. It's a beautiful evening. Go enjoy it."

With the dismissal from the table, Eugene would have to work to prolong the date, but Rosa was right. They stepped out into the warm summer evening, the street bustling with couples and groups and families enjoying it. Before they reached the bottom of the entry stairs, Ellie slipped her hand into Eugene's. *Maybe it won't be such hard work*, he thought, fighting back Paranoid Eugene, who wondered if the evening was going just a little too well.

"Can we go for a walk?" she asked.

Her hand was soft and warm in his. "Anywhere in particular?"

"Just a walk. Wherever."

"Wherever is good." Internally, Eugene told Paranoid Eugene to shut up.

They walked aimlessly, block after block, Eugene enjoying every minute and hoping Ellie did as well. She seemed to be, from that light laugh that erupted occasionally. As it grew dark, and the couple had wandered to the end of the commercial district, they turned back toward the restaurant.

In the sudden change of direction, Eugene noticed two people close on their heels, both in dark suits, their narrow black ties standing out against white shirts. They were easy to spot since there were very few people on the street at this time and at the edge of the hipster area. They weren't wearing sunglasses, but Eugene was sure they had them at hand.

"This doesn't look good," he said to Ellie.

"Do you know them?"

"No, but I think they know me." He directed her across the street and pulled her along as he started to jog.

The dark suits followed in pursuit.

"This way," said Ellie, tugging Eugene down a side alley.

"No, this is a..." They raced twenty paces into the darkness. "...dead end."

"Eugene Jones," called a voice from behind them.

"Yep, they know me," said Eugene.

"Eleanor Smith," commanded the other.

"What the..." Eugene grimaced at Ellie's form in the darkness next to him.

"Looks like they know me, too," she said.

Then Eugene looked over his shoulders. Yeah, both of them—one eyestalk curled over each shoulder—one eye focusing on each of the dark figures at the alley entrance. More important than what Ellie thought of him was looking out for her. Ellie turned to face their stalkers, and Eugene followed. They had to let go of each other's hand, but Ellie slipped her other hand, cool from the late evening, into Eugene's.

"What do you want?" asked Eugene in as gruff a voice as he could muster, which naturally dug up more of his Texas accent. The stalkers weren't phased by his words or his obvious alienness.

One advantage of having your eyes at the end of eighteen-inch stalks is it's easy to observe your own facial expression. Unfortunately, Eugene was giving his best fearsome, "I'm gonna eat you right after I rip off your head" look, and he could see that he wasn't selling it. He tried to stare them down, but judging from the sunglasses they now wore, that's probably exactly what they wanted.

From beside him, two bright blue flashes shot like laser pulses, one at each of the two dark figures blocking the alley. Their bodies collapsed as they absorbed the light beams.

"What the..." Eugene stared at the crumpled lumps.

"They're just stunned," said Ellie.

"Stunned?" *I'm stunned*, he thought. "They look—"

"*Really* stunned," she said. "Let's beat it before they remember why they came here tonight." She tugged on his hand to go, but his sluggishness and her momentum swung her around to face him. His eyes were safely back in their sockets. Hers glowed blue in the darkness, then faded while he watched.

"That blue. Blue lasers," said Eugene.

"Something like that," said Ellie. "We need to go. Now." She ran toward the alley entrance and Eugene let her pull him along with her.

"Who are they?" asked Eugene as they stepped around the dark, unconscious bodies.

"Bounty hunters, I think. Maybe federal agents. I don't—"

"Wait." Eugene stopped abruptly, yanking Ellie back around to face him. He could enjoy that view, side lit by the streetlamp, for a long time, but they didn't have that. Reluctantly, he let go of her hand to return to the closest collapsed body. He rifled through the jacket pockets. "Ah, there." The pen-like device was already in the now-victim's hand. "Take off the sunglasses and hold the eyes open," he said, fiddling with the device, looking for a switch, trying not to find it accidentally while pointed at himself.

"Like in the movies?"

"Like in the movies. Crazy, I know."

Eugene found what felt like a button switch. "Close your eyes." He positioned the device over the blank eyes Ellie had propped open and pressed the button. He could see the flash even through his double eyelids. Already familiar with the routine, they dispatched the second victim much quicker. "Clear," said Eugene before popping the flash.

When his eyelids stopped glowing, Eugene handed Ellie the device. The first one was already secure in his pant pocket.

"Should we?" she asked, holding the end of the device, but not taking it.

"I think we better."

She took it and slipped it into her clutch, holding it from the end like it might bite.

"Now, let's find our cars," said Eugene.

"We won't find mine. I walked."

"I thought you said…"

"I didn't say I drove."

Eugene couldn't remember her exact words from earlier. "No, you cleverly avoided the topic."

"I didn't want to explain that I don't have my license yet. I haven't been *here* long."

"Did you know I wasn't *from around here*?"

"No, but I was suspicious when Rosa directed me to your listing on the service."

"Rosa?!" Eugene stopped again to look at her. He could do that all night, but she might catch on to the ploy.

"I'd only been to the restaurant twice, and she took me in."

"Like she did me." *Ah, Rosa*, he reflected. Then in revelation, "Rosa! *We* are the covered dishes! The mocktinis were blue! The cannoli! Same color as your laser eyes."

"What are you talking about?" asked Ellie.

"I can explain on our second date."

"I hoped this one wasn't over yet."

About Covered Dishes

Covered Dishes began as a small concept, but grew into one of the longer stories and the basis for a few more. If you enjoyed *Covered Dishes*, look for *Lonely Cannoli: Alien Italian* (Rosa and Antonio's story) and *Electric Blue Mocktini: Alien Lightweight* (Ellie's story) in *Flashing Lights: Short and Weird Volume 2* (2024).

Prompt

Eyes at the end of eighteen-inch stalks would be a fantastic trait—unless you always have to hide it.

Inspiration

The working title was *Eyestalks are Overrated*. Although having eyestalks like Eugene's would be cool, Ellie's lasers are "way cooler."

For the backstory, I also drew on a childhood experience, eating at a local Italian restaurant my family frequented. The owners were so friendly and the food was delicious and affordable. With seven kids, we were that table others tried to avoid. One evening, a limo pulled up in front. Three men got out. One was an elderly gentleman in a dark suit. The other two were younger men, also in dark suits and wearing sunglasses. The gentleman was greeted with deference at the door and was directed to a quiet table. The two sunglassed men (yes, they wore them the entire time) stood by his table while the man enjoyed a full meal and read the newspaper. We later figured out who the man was when his picture appeared in the newspaper. My father's habit of never sitting with his back to the door had been affirmed.

Easter Eggs

The original draft of the story involved muggers in the alley, but I thought an homage to the classic "aliens are among us" movie series was appropriate, if not essential. I also included the requisite homage to *The Hitchhiker's Guide to the Galaxy*, which suggests that dolphins are the other sentient beings on Earth (and perhaps the more intelligent).

Hanky-Panky: Dirty Laundry

PG: Ghosts, Mainstream, Mystery

Terry held one argyle sock in her hand while searching for its match in the laundry basket, sea breeze scent rising from the basket with each toss of the clothes. Hopefully, it hadn't escaped. But Terry's perpetual laundry problem was with something appearing, not disappearing in each week's colors load. And it hadn't been a problem until Fred moved in.

Terry found the matched sock and folded the pair together on the dining table before she remembered, Fred rolled his military style. At least, he knew which direction to hang the toilet paper roll. *Something George never figured out.*

Thinking of George, Terry searched through the clothes in the basket. *Where is it?* Had her mysterious laundry crasher skipped a week? Had it finally slipped into the land of missing socks? She didn't want Fred to see it.

Speaking of Fred, he emerged from the hallway into the dining room, buttoning his cuffs as he walked. "I suggested we combine our laundry to save water, not to save me from doing laundry."

"It's fine." Terry rested her hands on top of the warm clothes. "I have the day off."

"But you did it last week, too."

And I'll continue to until I'm sure you won't find it. "You can do it next week. I promise."

The aroma of Fred's bodywash preceded him as he leaned toward her and they kissed. Terry usually loved the nutty shea butter smell, but it mingled strangely with the marine scented fabric softener. "I need to get to the office," he said, giving her another peck. "But next week is mine."

"Deal," she said.

As Fred turned toward the front door, Terry admired his thick, steel-gray hair, his straight back, the confident way he walked, the...

The corner of something light protruded from his pant cuff, trailing on the carpet. Terry was reminded of a day when she got to work and was holding her staff stand-up when someone noticed a drier sheet sticking out from her pant cuff. Fortunately, the team member waited until after the meeting to tell her, but how embarrassing.

And Terry, not Fred, was the one to be embarrassed now, too. This was not a drier sheet. It wasn't pink like the ones she used or white like the ones he had donated to their combined laundry supplies. It was the faded tartan of dark and light blue and white Terry had been searching for, and she couldn't let him walk out with it. "Fred," she said, trying not to sound alarmed. "Just a sec."

Fred stopped and turned. "What's up? Did I forget something?"

"No." Terry tried not to dash to him. She bent down and yanked the patterned cloth from his pants. "Just something stuck in your pantleg." She wadded it up, but her hand was too small to conceal it.

"I hadn't noticed. Thanks. That could be embarrassing." He almost turned to walk out, but hesitated. "What is it?"

"Probably just a drier sheet. It's happened to me. You're right. Embarrassing." She turned back toward the dining room. "Have a nice day," she said, or mostly said, through the cracks in her voice.

Terry felt Fred's hand on her shoulder. "What is it, Terry?" By "it" he might have meant the swatch of cloth, but by his concerned tone, he meant more.

Terry opened her fist, letting the cloth unfurl in her hand, a rare blue flower that Fred plucked from her palm. The cloth opened fully as it drifted past Terry's head.

"A man's handkerchief?" said Fred.

And, by "man," he meant "another man" because Fred didn't have any handkerchiefs.

"It was George's," said Terry. The one she had cried into at his funeral. But Fred couldn't know this. She hadn't met him until years later.

"I see," said Fred, stepping around Terry, holding the handkerchief so the monogram was exposed, looking past it into Terry's clouding eyes. "It must come as a shock."

"Yes, it does." *It always does. Even after all these years. All the times it has appeared in my laundry.*

Fred placed the handkerchief in Terry's hand. "Are you okay?" he asked.

"I'll be fine."

"How do you suppose it got into the clothes?"

"I just opened a box of old clothes. Was washing them before donating them." *Not a lie.* "It might have been mixed in with those." *It might have been, but wasn't.*

"I guess so."

Terry stroked Fred's arm and stepped past him. "I should throw it away."

"Are you sure?"

"It's just an old hanky."

"If that's what you want. You don't have to. I understand."

Terry stepped on the foot pedal of the kitchen trash can, the lid flipped up, and she dropped the old hanky in, where it sat on top of the coffee grounds she had dumped to make their morning cup. "No, it's time I moved on." She lifted her foot. The lid closed with a "thump."

They were both quiet a moment before Terry said, "You should probably get going. You'll be late for work."

"I could... OK. I'll get going." He started toward the door, then turned around. "I'll call when I'm leaving. I'll pick up something for dinner."

"That would be nice." Though Terry hadn't eaten breakfast, she couldn't think about eating, but what to prepare for dinner was one less thing she had to think about. She heard the "thud" of the door closing behind her.

When Terry finished folding her socks and rolling Fred's and putting them in their drawers, the shock of the morning's events and her skipped breakfast settled in her unsettled stomach. Thinking a banana would satisfy both and save her any dirty dishes, Terry ate one for lunch before she realized she would have to throw away the peel.

Terry eased her foot down on the pedal. The trash can lid eased open. And the hanky lay atop the trash. Fortunately, the coffee grounds were from two mornings before and were dry and hadn't soaked into the hanky. Not that it mattered. The hanky, along with the coffee grounds and her banana peel, would end up in a landfill soon enough. But she couldn't throw the slimy banana peel in on top.

Terry lifted the hanky out of the trash by the corner, gently shaking a shower of coffee grounds from it, before tossing in the banana peel.

I won't mind doing the laundry another week, thought Terry. She tossed the hanky in with a load still in the wash cycle. The washer's digital display went dark, flashed brightly, then returned to normal. "Or two."

About Hanky-Panky

As with several of the *Flashing Lights* stories, I tried to maintain plausible supernatural and mundane explanations for the hanky in the laundry. Was Terry's rescue of the hanky from the trash the first time she had put it in the laundry, or is that how it got there all the time? If you enjoyed *Hanky-Panky*, look for *Hanging On: Life Goes On* in *Flashing Lights: Short and Weird Volume 2* (2024).

Prompt

What if something keeps *appearing* in the wash, specifically, a widow's deceased husband's hanky?

Inspiration

There's this old mystery of where socks go when they disappear from the laundry. As with several of the Flashing Lights stories, I flipped this trope on its head.

And yes, I have had a dryer sheet escape my pant leg during a team standup.

The Dragon of Dalhart: A Dustbowl Tale

G: Folktale, Historical, Serious, YA

Christian was with Father, and Mother was in the house when the dragon rose in the far distance. There was just a black line rising along the horizon, but Eva knew what it was. She had been filling the pail at the cistern when a gust of wind whipped the bundle of her hair around into her eyes, causing her to look up from the water flowing into the pail, and to squint into the wind pouring over her. The black line grew taller, like a wall, filling the gap between the ground and the setting sun, hiding the pale gray-pink evening sky behind its blackness.

The dragon of Dalhart rose from the earth.

The pail was only half filled, so Eva pumped the handle again. Mother said a full pail. No being lazy, or Eva would have to walk out here and fill it again. Though, with the dragon flying toward the house, Mother would not send Eva to the pump again today.

But Mother needed the water in the house. A full pail.

Eva pumped the handle again as Christian and Father ran along the fence line toward the house. Explosions of powdery earth flew from their every step like shooting comets.

When Christian opened the door to go into the house and out of the wind, the door swung free of his hand and slammed against the wall with a bang that rattled the one window. No sooner had Christian heaved it closed, the door flew open again.

Mother, in her white dirndl, stood in the black square of the door-way, yelling in her strictest German for Eva to come in. "Right now, Eva!"

While Mother stood there, the dragon's shadow fell on the house, heavy and cold and sudden, like a winter night.

Fighting her fear, Eva looked back to see the dragon's many long necks and slender heads writhing in the darkness, swallowing the sun. Lightning flashed from its angry mouth and eyes, striking the ground and shattering the black sky in constant crimson arcs as the dragon's roar filled her ears.

The dragon raced toward Eva.

The pail was full now. Too full, as Eva lifted it and walked quickly, then tried to run, toward the house without spilling any of the precious water.

It was Christian who told Eva these wicked winds were not storms. They were the attacks of a monster. The dragon of Dalhart. Mother said not to believe him. "It is not a dragon," she had said. But now, Mother screamed at Eva to hurry into the house as Eva slowed to look over her shoulder at the dragon.

As Eva approached the house, the storm of the dragon's rage rained on her head and against her back, and within two steps, it was pouring. But it was dirt that pelted Eva, not water. She hunched over the pail as she ran to keep the dirt out of the water, but through the surge surrounding her, she couldn't see the precious liquid that slopped onto her feet with each lurching step.

The dragon was swallowing Eva before she could reach the safety of the house.

Someone gripped Eva's arm. It was Father's big hand. And his other was on her back, pushing her along to keep up with his long strides. And someone held her hand that held the pail, helping her carry it, the wire handle now pressing painfully into her palm. There were voices yelling as they ran, but the dragon's roar was louder, and the words sounded like the dull thuds of their feet on the shifting earth.

Eva's feet left the ground, but she was still running when they landed on something hard and flat. In four more steps, the door banged shut behind her, and the wind stopped pressing on her back and whipping her hair and tearing at her dirndl.

The dragon slammed against the door and the wall and the window to get at her.

"What were you thinking, Eva?" cried Mother in German.

"You don't like me to spill," said Eva. "We will need a full pail to last until the dragon leaves."

"There is no dragon." Mother's voice was full of scorn, but her eyes fell on Christian. "I don't know who is the greater fool, you or your brother."

Mother's scolding startled to a stop when the dragon attacked the house, bending its walls and rattling its boards and banging the metal sheets of its roof. It breathed dirt through every crack and seam into the house, scattering the lamplight in a sparkling haze.

Eva's wide eyes darted to Christian. He understood. He knew more than mother. "It's the dragon of Dalhart," he mouthed.

Christian was two years older and one year smarter, and knew about dragons, the beasts who dwelt in mountain caves. He was born in the mountains of Germany, like in the picture on the wall Mother touched every night in the lamplight before trimming the wick and going to bed in the darkness. But other than the grainy picture, Eva had never seen mountains, only the vast flatness around the house that Father, his eyes bright with hope, called the "Great Plains," the only English words he'd say when it was just the four of them.

Mother rested her hand on Eva's head and stroked her hair. "Shake the dirt from your clothes, and brush your hair," she said. Then she soaked scraps of linen with water from the pail, carefully wringing them over the washbasin to catch the pearly beads, then pressed the scraps into the cracks around the window and door to block the dragon's fury from entering the house, while Father nailed wooden braces across the flexing door, the thuds of the hammer barely heard over the banging of the roof.

While Eva brushed her hair, Christian whispered to her in English so Mother wouldn't understand. "They tried to bury the dragon in his cave by filling it with dirt. But a hundred and one kobolds dug him out."

At the familiar word, Mother corrected Christian in German, shaking her finger at him. "No kobolds, Christian. Stop scaring your sister."

"That's what I said," he lied in German. "Not to worry, Eva. There are no kobolds."

When Mother looked away, Christian pointed at Eva's favorite book, the only one she could call her own, *Grimm's Fairy Tales*. He had opened it to *Die vier kunstreichen Brüder*, *The Four Clever Brothers*. Eva stared at the drawing of the dragon there, recognizing the long, snakey necks and those red eyes she had seen in the clouds when she had looked back and Mother yelled.

Christian tapped the pad of his forefinger on the page, on the dragon, which wriggled with the jouncing of each tap. "The dragon brings the eternal night that lives with him in his cave. And all the dirt they poured on top of him. He will bury us with it."

"What about the lightning?" asked Eva.

"He breathes lightning," said Christian in a hoarse whisper, just loud enough for Eva to hear over the dragon's roar. "He's a lectric dragon."

"What's lectric?" Eva looked around the room, hoping the dragon's lectric breath and lightning gaze couldn't enter the house, couldn't get through its shivering boards or past the wet linen scraps spread across its cracks.

"We don't have any lectric. Like the lights at school and the lightning in a storm and the dragon of Dalhart's breath."

"What is he telling you, Eva?" asked Mother, still pressing damp scraps into the gaps.

Eva didn't know what lectric was. "I don't know the word in German," she said, shielding Christian from Mother's scorn. "Something from school."

"Good, you two study your school."

Which Mother always had to tell Christian, but never Eva, because she loved school. Except now, she wasn't so sure since school had lectric.

When the dragon left and they dug out from the dirt and Eva was back at school, she would ask about lectric. For now, she would read about the dragon of *The Four Clever Brothers* in the lamplit haze of the kitchen, while the dragon of Dalhart attacked the house.

April 14, 1935, "Black Sunday." Dalhart, Texas

About The Dragon of Dalhart

The Dragon of Dalhart is the least speculative of the *Flashing Lights* stories, but I believe it fits in the collection and will appeal to many readers. Fairy/Folk tales once served to caution children of danger, so I thought a modern folk tale invented by the character Christian would be a fun way to warn Eva of the danger posed by the dust storm. In the end, although Eva feared the dragon, she may have been even more frightened had she known the truth.

Prompt

What kind of modern folk tale could warn a child of such an unusual event like "Black Sunday"?

Inspiration

I wrote *The Dragon of Dalhart* while sitting in my RV, rocking with the wind, in Dalhart, Texas. Inspirations for the story include photographs of Black Sunday available in the National archives and the book *The Worst Hard Time: The Untold Story of Those Who Survived the Great American Dust Bowl* by Timothy Egan.

Easter Egg

While all the characters and accounts in the story are fictional, the character Christian is an homage to my friend and fellow fantasy RPG creator Christian Eichhorn of Germany. Christian and I coauthored a roleplaying adventure for children titled *101 Koboldz* (2019).

Freak Magnet: Strange Attraction

PG: Aliens, Humorous, Mainstream, Sci-Fi

Left Bookend: Abduction Coordinator

George was sitting in the Taurus, listening to classic ELO with the window rolled up, while I filled the tank with mid-grade. I was inserting the nozzle when, from behind me, I heard, "Hey, howsit goin'?"

I didn't recognize the voice, so my radar started pinging. You might think my cringe was premature or an overreaction, but you'll see. My radar might be sensitive, but from years of testing, it's spot on. And it was the second time it had gone off today.

I turned toward the pump where the voice had originated. The guy on the other side of the island was standing next to the pump, leaning with his shoulder against it.

"Hey," I said. "Good. Thanks. You?"

"I'm good, man. You live 'round here?"

"Not far. Yeah. You need directions to somewhere?"

"You sound like my mom. No, man. Just wond'rin' if you saw the lights last night."

This guy was in at least his thirties, so I wondered why his mom was still giving him directions. Though he talked like he was stoned, I didn't smell anything but gas fumes, which is unusual these days. No, his eyes were clear and wide and staring right into mine.

"Lights?" I looked away and searched for the window squeegee as an excuse to move away.

"Yeah, man. Up on the hill." From the corner of my eye, I could see him pointing toward the mountainside across the highway. "Over there," he said louder and pointed more dramatically to get my attention.

"Didn't see it." *I had.* "Was it cool?" *I just had to ask...*

"Sh-yeah, it was cool. I was setting up my gear to watch the grand alignment and nearly forgot what I was doing."

"Grand alignment?" The words were out before I could help myself. Okay, so maybe I am partly responsible for these diversions.

"Yeah. You know, the planetary alignment. Five planets; Mercury, Venus, Mars, Jupiter, and Saturn all—"

"Oh, *that* grand alignment," I interrupted. "Of course." I had only a vague idea of what he was talking about, but wanted to move on. "I thought you were talking about the new Netflix series. Or is it Amazon?"

"I wouldn't know. I just watch my YouTube. Is it any good?"

I figured as much. There's a YouTube channel for everyone, which is why it's always "my" YouTube. "Dunno. I don't watch either."

"Watch tonight. The sky, I mean." He pointed back to the hillside. "'Bout three a.m. in the morning. Maybe it'll happen again."

"Yeah. I will. Thanks."

"The grand alignment will still be good, too. Hey! You want to come over?" This is where the conversation was headed from his first "hey." "We can check out M1 in my Schmidt Cassegrain while we wait." He nodded toward the minimart and offered, "I could get some snacks. If my mom was still alive, she would bake—"

"Sorry. Can't. Got company tonight," I said, pointing a thumb toward the passenger side of the car where I knew George would be pointing back or making faces. Or both. I didn't look. He was only along as far as picking up his car at the shop that evening, but it isn't lying when it isn't their business, right? "Thanks though."

The click of his pump handle snapping closed sent relief through my ears and down my spine.

"No problem," he said. "Later."

"Later." *I hope not.* "Sorry about your mom."

"Thanks. That was a year ago. I'm good. Tough living alone, though."

Definitely seeing him later. I was wondering if he had moved up from the basement yet when I heard the beeps of the pump as he closed his transaction. Then the squeak of his door hinge. "Be safe," he said, using the phrase that had replaced all other forms of "farewell" in the last few years.

"Now *you* sound like *my* mom," I chided. He paused all movement there, half in, half out of his car. *Too soon?* I could only see one foot on the pavement and half a calf, so leaned to get a clear view of his face past the pump—the definitive portrayal of *bewilderment*. "You too," I said, unsticking him, knowing neither he nor I nor either of our mom's had any say in the matter. He had been swept into my field. He had seen the light, as it were. "Safe" was not an option.

When I reached the passenger window with the squeegee, George was pointing at me through the glass and laughing. I slapped the dripping sponge edge against the window, concealing George's face behind a soapy spatter, then scrubbed that window extra hard before moving on. I tried not to smile at George's dramatic frown two inches from the glass.

"What'd your friend have to say?" asked George before my left foot had even cleared the door jamb.

"He wanted to know if I'd seen the grand alignment—five planets at three a.m. *in the morning*. Not to be confused with the TV series."

"I haven't seen three a.m. in the morning or otherwise since I quit bartending."

I was counting on that, which is why I didn't bother to mention the lights on the mountain.

George laughed as he mimicked the guy pointing toward the mountaintop. "You're such a freak magnet."

It's true. For as long as I can remember, I've attracted the attention of people who seem a little weird. George says it's because I'm attracted to them—I engage them, make eye contact, that sort of thing. But in many cases, like the guy at the gas station, I didn't even know he was there until he got caught in my freak magnet field.

"It's this town," I said, evading. "Full of freaks, so there's plenty of opportunity to bump into a few." Which is why I hung around here as long as I had.

"Only happens when I'm with you."

"I could say the same."

"And you'd be lying. Everyone sees it."

"It could happen to anyone."

"Maybe could, but doesn't. That's your second close encounter today."

"Counting you?" I said as we merged into traffic.

The first was during lunch at a local eatery. George and I were enjoying a burger and a beer—a giant mushroom *burger*, no bun, and a hard seltzer in George's case, but we had quit quibbling over terminology shortly after we met.

It was almost three years ago now that I moved here. George was the first local I met and the only one who I had managed to keep close. He was a special kind of strange, but couldn't hold a candle to my freak followers. Another quibble he had won handily months ago. If I told George why I was really here, he would argue that it was his company and quibbling that kept me from moving on. To be fair to him and honest with myself, it was why I enjoyed it.

We were enjoying our *beers* when the host seated someone at the next table. We were waiting for our food... not a third to join the conversation, when we heard, "Nice afternoon."

It was the same voice I heard moments earlier, asking to be seated "over there." The one that was a little high and a lot screechy—what people describe as fingernails on a chalkboard. But I've never seen a chalkboard, much less heard fingernails on one, so couldn't say. From the sounds I've heard compared to it, though, I can be thankful for that, at least. Irritating as it was, the screechiness wasn't what pinged my radar halfway across the room.

Maybe unsure if we had heard the first time, the fingernails made another trip down the chalkboard. "Yep. A nice afternoon."

"A delightful afternoon," said George. He tapped my shin with his toe, nudging me with that shroom-eating grin. "Idn't it?" George doesn't have the radar like I do, but knows when mine pings, and loves to create an echo.

"Yeah, nice," I agreed.

"Good day for rock hunting," mused the chalkboard.

"I'll bet," said George.

"With the freeze and thaw of the spring and a warm sunny day... Yep. Great rock hunting day."

"First time out this year?" asked George.

"This spring, yep."

"Good day for it," said George.

"Yep, good day for rock hunting."

Before we knew it, the rock hunter—who George later dubbed the "rock whisperer"—was seated at our table. At least we were offered Asiago truffle fries as a consolation. Though George and I both are off the fries.

We heard all about rock hunting, the types of rocks, minerals, and gems—apparently, there's a difference—found in the area, and the locations of all the shops in the region where we could go to rockhound meetups, and buy precious... rocks. Even ones found by the humble hunter honoring our table.

We were assured that mother nature unearthed the nuggets. (I'm sure I misused the term—these conversations were always loaded with technical terms). The rockhound only collected and separated the "specimens" from the "matrix." Though I hadn't a clue what "separated from the matrix" meant, it made the most sense of anything in the conversation. The entire process sounded eerily familiar.

When we finished eating, the server graciously brought our checks at the same time, so we might leave together. I think she was on to the situation and was just being a pain, but her smile was so practiced it was indiscernible from genuine.

The rock whisperer followed us out to the Taurus and pointed toward the mountainside, offering to show us where to find unusual *specimens*—the special rocks that aren't part of the matrix, I guessed. "Right up there."

But we declined. We had a busy day ahead. *We didn't.* Actually, we were going to play classic *Space Invaders* and *Defender* on George's custom console for a few hours while waiting for his car. "Some other time." *No, never.* "Maybe we'll find you at one of those meetups." *That we'd never attend.* "Have a great day rock hunting." *Truly, have a great day.* "Be safe."

When I said the stoner at the gas pump was second and the rock whisperer was first, that was only true as far as George knew, and as I would openly admit. But there had been two earlier, before I picked up George at his apartment. There was the septuagenarian putting a flier for furniture slipcovers in my door when I tried to leave. Apparently, I wasn't aware of the horrible germs I was exposing myself to by sitting in my same old chair every evening. Though George sat in it sometimes, I felt it was pretty safe without the easily sanitized, waterproof, non-porous, non-fading, hypoallergenic, sweat-sticking plastic.

Then there was the fellow coin-dropper at the laundromat, wearing sweats that needed laundering more than anything in my load. And I was pushing the expiration date on my never-leaves-the-house tee. I could only imagine the clothes worthy of a wash and dry in those baskets. Once the clothes were done, this person was going camping up on the mountain—though the finger was pointing toward downtown. But who am I to correct? I'm not local.

I excused myself by feigning I had forgotten a load at home and dashed to the car before I even learned what passion fired up this freak. To be fair, from the *Call of Duty* tee and Blizzard Entertainment logo on the sweats, I didn't need to share more time or words to figure it out. What on Earth would compel this nerd to go camping?

George's term "freak" might be unfair—more like overly, intensely, single-mindedly, ceaselessly passionate about a single topic. Like how a seven-year-old is about dinosaurs. Only twenty or thirty or sixty years older than seven. With all those years of dedication and distance from anyone who might have been close. An aficionado. A savant. A loner. A nerd. A geek. A freak.

So, at dusk, with four encounters, you might say it had been a stellar day for freak finding. And there they all were, milling around a meadow on the mountain where they had each pointed—or thought they had pointed. (That one must have hitched a ride with someone who knew their directions). Oh, and the woman who had bumped her grocery cart into mine that evening, but I really wasn't expecting to see her here. She had been barely a blip.

It was quite the social hour up there as the sky grew dark and they all talked about their passions without a moment's silence to listen to one another. About midnight, when the stargazing was getting good, and the light flashed high overhead, I ducked behind a huge rock—from my lunchtime lecture, I'm sure it was gneiss.

I held my breath and waited for the whirring sound. *There it is.* Then the "pop-pop-pop" of blinding light and ear-splitting pressure. *Yep.* By now, I knew to close my eyes and cover my ears for this part. Then the "whoosh" and the trees bending in the breeze. *Cool.*

My phone buzzed. That would be my offshore bank, alerting me to the deposit. What good is natural talent if it can't pay the bills?

About Freak Magnet

Freak Magnet is the left bookend of the *Abduction Coordinator* bookend series. Be sure to read the right bookend of the series later in this collection to get the full picture.

Prompt

What if my propensity to attract peculiar people isn't an accident? And could be useful?

Inspiration

The inspiration for *Freak Magnet* is simply, I am one. For as long as I can remember. The "rock whisperer" was a real encounter (though it was at a gas station like the first encounter here). The guy would not let me go, followed me to my car door. My brother was in the car laughing when I got in, knowing what had happened. We called him the "rock whisperer."

To be clear here, there was nothing medically wrong with the guy. He was intelligent and articulate. He was just over-passionate about his hobby and assumed I would be too. I used the word freak as a synonym for stoner here also, which was the common lingo "back in my day."

I don't know why I cause this attraction, but I assure you I'm not assisting aliens in abducting humans for research. We finished that research ages ago.

Easter Egg

Naturally, I had to poke fun at my "hometown," the Colorado front range, for its abundance of freaks.

Souls at Sea: A Bermuda Training Voyage

PG: Aliens, Ghosts, Historical, Humorous, Sci-Fi

Left Bookend: Age of Sail in Space

Royal Naval Dockyard, Bermuda, 31 January 1880

Captain Stirling stopped pacing when he heard the bosun's whistle, followed by a knock on his cabin door. "Enter."

Mate Adamson opened the door and stood there at attention. "Ready to launch, Captain."

"Those landlubbers stop retching long enough to set sail?"

Adamson grimaced and replied with a tentative, "Aye, Captain."

The much anticipated news wasn't necessarily welcome to either of them. Stirling had recently taken command of the cranky, old sixth-rate frigate. With her new name, HMS *Atalanta*, came a new crew, nearly three hundred mostly seasick lads. To call this a training voyage suggested there were enough able seamen aboard to school them.

We'll never make Falmouth alive, thought Sterling. England lay half a world away, and though Stirling had made the crossing many times, it seemed more distant than ever.

"Let's get under way, then," said Stirling. "And hope we don't make a mess of it. Right behind you."

Adamson saluted and left the door ajar for the captain. A moment later, the bosun piped on the whistle again.

"May God have mercy on our souls," said Stirling as he stepped into the chaos of scurrying lads on the main deck.

$$\bullet \; \bullet \; \bullet \; \bullet \bullet \; \bullet \bullet \; \bullet \; \bullet \; \bullet$$

After two weeks of foundering, rolling to near capsize, and missing stays, the ship was less than a week's voyage beyond Bermuda, but the young crew was learning the ship and her ways.

Stirling looked through the glass at their first true test.

"Seen anything like it before?" asked Adamson.

Not in my... thought Stirling, but he didn't respond. He had seen many a squall and tropical storm, but nothing so perfect. The rotating cylinder of cloud and sea drawn together in midair was about a mile across and black as a hole in the sky. "This is as close a look as we want to get. Navigate around it."

"We've tried, Captain."

"These lads forget their lessons already? Shaken by a little storm?"

"Some are getting scared, but they've executed well."

"The problem, then?"

"The storm moved with us. We tacked to the north, then the south. It stayed straight ahead. And now we're coming upon it."

"And if we turned about?"

"I'm not suggesting we—"

"Well, I am, Adamson. There are too many young souls aboard to sail this old crank through a storm like that. Turn about."

"Aye, aye, Captain."

The sails snapped taught. The *Atalanta* listed hard as she might. The sun swung from port to starboard. And the storm stayed dead ahead.

"Drop sheets and hang tight," said Stirling. "Give the order." He added, "Be quick," but Adamson was already barking the orders.

As the sails luffed and the crew lashed them to their spars, the *Atalanta* slowed to a bobbing stop on the rising waves. But the storm approached ever faster.

"All hands to the pumps and pails. Anyone on deck needs a belay line. That includes you, Adamson."

On Adamson's orders, the crew scrambled to their stations—some, their quarters—their fear rising with the tide around them.

Just as the sea-cloud wall was upon them, a hole opened in it. The sea and foam raced over an arch, forming a tunnel into the darkness. When the storm passed over the ship, the arch collapsed behind it, sealing the whirling wall to the surface of the sea. For all the torrent about them, the deck was dead calm.

Lights of various colors flashed overhead like stars pulled close. Stirling raised the glass and scanned the overhead. "It's metallic. A structure. I dare say it's a ship of some unearthly kind. Something of Verne's imagination."

A blue-white arc of lightning illuminated a structure protruding from the bottom of the smooth surface. The arc climbed the structure from its tip a hundred feet above the mainmast to a dark hole opening in the smooth surface at its base, three hundred feet or more above *that*.

"Like Jacob's ladder, inviting us to the heavens."

• • • ● ●• ● ● •• •

Captain FzZboP paced the bridge of her ship, *NZd!R#*, waiting to hear if the transfer of Earthlings to the specimen cage was complete. Six lyrps out from home with a shipload of trainees, she had about worn a slot in the bridge between her command console and the main screen.

With a "bing," a purple light flashed on the teleporter console. She stopped pacing, resting on her back leg while rubbing her front two together to make a persistent "chirp."

"Transfer complete, Captain," said LrGelD, reporting what was obvious from the console alert, but it was his job to report such things.

"We caught them all?"

"Aye, Captain. Two hundred, eighty-seven specimens."

"Good job, LrGelD. Let's—"

LrGelD interrupted. "Slight problem, Captain."

"Slight? Explain."

"All specimens are accounted for in the cage, but..."

"Speak up."

"They're also on the wooden vessel."

"How so?"

"They have souls, Captain. Or should I say, 'had.'"

"We've taken plenty of other samples from this stupid planet. None had souls."

"All the same, Captain. The bodies are healthy and walking about in their cage—though they don't seem interested in the hay. But their souls are down on that vessel. In fact, they appear to be preparing it for travel."

"Training mission or not, the council will be pissed."

"More than pissed, Captain. They'll take your ship."

"Then collect those souls."

"We can't. Our equipment isn't—"

"Squish them back together, then?"

"Nope. No can do."

"What we *no-can-do* is have two hundred plus disembodied souls roaming the planet. We're supposed to be incognito." FzZboP returned to pacing, spinning around on her three legs, two hands scratching her chin, one wiping sweat from her eyebrow, the claws of the other three snapping in staccato. "Suggestions?"

"Set them loose somewhere else."

"Where?"

LrGelD craned his jointed neck to look straight up, as if to see past the vented metallic acoustic ceiling.

"The whole wooden... thingy?"

"Souls and all."

"Won't they suffocate?"

"They'll be fine. Souls don't need air."

FzZboP didn't know if that was true, but wasn't going to waste precious time or energy debating it. "Brilliant, LrGelD. Make it so."

LrGelD fiddled with the transporter controls. The wooden "thingy," souls and all, disappeared from below. A blip blinked and bleeped on his screen, scanning the void above the planet.

"All good?"

"Yep. They're off and moving away from the planet. I applied a shield so their vessel doesn't break up."

"Despite the hiccup, this was a good fishing spot. Mark it on the map."

"Coordinates set, Captain."

"If they taste good, we'll come back."

About Souls at Sea

Souls at Sea was one of the original concepts for the *Flashing Lights* series, inspiring parts of the series cover. One of my favorite aspects of *Souls at Sea* and its companion bookend story is the thread that ties them together across time and space. Be sure to read the right bookend of the *Age of Sail in Space* bookend series later in this collection to get the full picture.

Since the concept for the right bookend story came first, this prompt already had the wind in its sails.

Prompt

How might an age of sail ship end up traveling through space? Alien abduction at the Bermuda Triangle, of course!

Inspiration

I started developing the story by researching ships that went missing near Bermuda in the late 1800s and discovered the story of the training ship HMS *Atalanta*. The true story was perfect as a setup for my fantastical finish.

The account in *Souls at Sea* of HMS *Atalanta*, its crew, departure conditions, and disappearance of the ship are historical. Although the tragic incident has often been used as evidence of the Bermuda Triangle phenomenon, the remains of a wrecked ship discovered near the Azores on April 19, 1880, are believed to have been the *Atalanta*.

One of my favorite aspects of *Souls at Sea* was the collision of two very different sailing missions with ill-prepared trainees aboard.

Shannon's Eleven: The Cold Get Hot

PG: Ghosts, Humorous, Mainstream

As Fred walked into the casino from the valet, he was struck by the ruckus of the machines and the chill of the AC. These were as expected as was the grimace of the manager there to meet him.

"Can we discuss the *problem* in my office?" asked the obviously distraught man.

Fred looked around at the crowd occupied with their conversations, engrossed with their cards, or absorbed into their machines. "No one is listening to us except your security team. Tell me now if we need to hide anything from them."

The manager looked around the room, inadvertently pointing out the hidden camera locations with his gaze. "No, they are fully aware of the *problem*. I was thinking more about the guests."

This guy was jumpier than most, and would be a dead give-away that something was wrong. If anyone cared to look up from their machines or the tables.

"Why? Do I stand out in my black jeans and double-ex-ell baseball jersey?" Fred had seen at least a dozen men in similar attire. The manager should have been more concerned about guys wearing a certain black and silver NFL jersey. Ah, but they were the home team now. "The 'Specters' could be a team in any small town. You just noticed it because I told you to look for it. Just walk like we're having a casual conversation and show me what concerns you." Funny, they never asked about his player number, "2," which should be the manager's actual concern. Number "1" should be along any minute.

"You noticed how cold it is in here."

"Yeah, felt good. It's a scorcher out there today." After ten meetings like this, Fred had to get creative with his schtick to avoid getting bored.

"Not so good that guests are wearing their coats at the tables."

"A blocked AC vent?" Fred knew it wasn't, but had to string the manager along to earn his pay.

"The AC is turned off."

"Saving on operational expenses, then. What else is odd?"

They walked past a block of machines that were cordoned off with velvet ropes and hanging signs that said "Cleaning" and "Cuidado." "These machines are paying out higher than programmed, so we blocked them off."

"And they check out ok otherwise, I assume."

"Yes. There's nothing wrong mechanically or with the software."

The manager showed Fred a roulette wheel, a bank of poker tables, and two craps tables also cordoned off. All paying out at extraordinary percentages. The roulette wheel just bore signs in plexi table tents on the table and at the center of the wheel saying "Table Closed." It was the latest game to go awry, and the casino had run out of chrome stanchions and purple velvet rope.

Earning his keep and enjoying how the questions annoyed the manager, Fred asked about the "normal" actions taken to validate the equipment and ensure no one was cheating. "You always have some areas closed for cleaning or slow times anyway, so what's the big deal?"

"The *problem* has been moving through the casino. We never know when or where until it is too late. Or when we can re-open an area. If we can at all."

"Oh, yeah. You could have opened those poker tables there at least a week ago." Fred didn't know that, but he knew casino managers hated lost opportunity, and egged the guy on.

"You know the *problem,* then?"

Fred was tired of the way the manager said "problem," but he was almost done, anyway. "It's not unusual for someone who has *passed from this life* to blame all their worldly troubles on a particular machine or table or even a dealer. But they're dead, so can never win. But... some find solace by retaliating. You have an especially pissed off specter here. Either they lost at everything in the house or they wanted to get back at the casino, not just the machine or table. You really should treat your guests better."

The manager straightened his posture, which had become more slouched the more they toured the closed sections. "We treat our guests the finest." At least the whiner showed a little spunk.

The two had reached the very back of the casino, to the discount buffet entrance. Fred sniffed, enjoying the hit of ginger and garlic, then nodded toward the line of guests waiting to be seated. "You haven't had anyone get uh..." Fred made a sickly face and stuck out his tongue.

"No!" The manager took Fred's arm and spun him to walk the opposite direction.

"That's fortunate. Never cheat guests on their meals. Trust me. You don't want that kind of retaliation. Whew."

The manager lost a step as he shuddered at the thought.

It was true but rare that a specter would injure a casino by attacking its guests, but it takes all sorts to fill a casino, and you never know who will come back to get back. As a habitual casino diner, though, Fred did his part to guarantee quality food. That possibility would surely be a topic at the next casino owners' Rotary meeting.

A shout of glee reached them over the monotony of bings and pings. "Woo-hoo! I won it! I won! One pull. Wooooo-hooooo. Yeah!"

Fred's eyes followed the rainbow of flashing lights across the casino hall. He couldn't see its end, but he knew where to find the pot of gold.

The manager finally stood erect and lurched toward the front of the casino, like coming out of the starting blocks. Fred grabbed his arm, but tried not to squeeze too hard.

"Cool down. That should be the last of your long odds pay outs." Fred took his cell phone from his pocket. "You'll receive my invoice in your email right about..."

The manager's phone buzzed in his pocket.

"Now."

"That's it? You didn't do anything. And while you wandered around asking stupid questions, the *problem* struck again."

"Oh, I did something, all right. I cleaned them out. Apparently, they just wanted to hit you one last time on the way out the door." Fred nodded toward the entrance. "One for the road, you might say. You have thirty days to pay, so you have time to verify that the *problem* is gone."

"What did you do? I didn't see anything..."

"If I told you, you'd tell all your casino buddies at the Rotary Club and I'd be out of business." His fellow Rotarians were likely where the manager heard about Fred's service.

"How'd you know I belong..."

Fred was baffled by how someone wearing a pin declaring what he does for kicks could be surprised when Fred showed he knew. It was the power of suggestion, thinking Fred's special insight extended to the mundane. "All you need to know is you're back in full operation."

"Really? We can open these tables? The slots and poker machines?"

"Open everything as quickly as you please. Your *problem* is gone. And I'll be going." Fred turned to leave and when the manager fell in behind him, he stopped, so the manager almost ran into him. "It's warming up in here already. You'll have to turn that AC on tomorrow."

The manager held his hands out to sample the air temperature, and while he was looking up at the AC vents overhead, Fred started walking again.

With the manager close on his heels, Fred passed a woman at the giant slot machine near the entrance, surrounded by other guests. The lights on the machine were still flashing and the bells still ringing as casino employees collected her information. "What's your last name again, Esmeralda?" She was still covering her mouth, crying, and jumping up and down with joy.

Fred walked past the crowd, leaving the manager to his crew, and without giving the jubilant woman a second look. He'd see Shannon back at home. She looked good as a brunette. Too bad she couldn't keep it that way for a few days.

Honestly, Fred didn't know how Shannon convinced the disgruntled specters to let her take one last big payout on their behalf, then leave their haunt. Must be something in that fae ancestry she claimed, but Fred didn't think too hard on it. Shannon was the medium. He was just an extra-large distraction.

But at eleven payouts, eleven phantom partners, their jig might be up. Although they, really Shannon, provided a legitimate service—the destructive specters did leave—but the casinos might not appreciate the payment method, the way he and Shannon cashed out. Walking away from the table might be the best move now, but then what would they do for entertainment?

About Shannon's Eleven

As with the Sherlock Holmes stories, sometimes a story is best told from the viewpoint of the accomplice. Though we follow Fred through the casino, he's just a grifter. A good one, but Shannon is the master thief and apparently has a fae way of convincing ghosts to let her get back at the casinos on their behalf. *Shannon's Eleven* is intended to be just pure fun.

Prompt

What if ghosts of loser gamblers retaliate on casinos by fixing the odds? And a couple of thieves make bank on the supernatural animosity.

Inspiration

The inspiration for *Shannon's Eleven* should be obvious—I, not so cleverly, included part of it in the title. The premise of the story is essentially, *Ghostbusters* meets *Ocean's Eleven*.

Shannon's Eleven was originally published with the title *Long Odds*, but I changed it so readers knew better what to expect.

Christmas Angel: Leaning Into Christmas

G: Holiday, Humorous, Mainstream, YA

The angel at the top of my Christmas tree smiled down at me. Miraculously, she perched there, bolt upright. I say miraculously because in the twentyish years I had placed her there, always careful to stand her straight, trimming the treetop to prop her up, by the time I finished decorating the rest of the tree, she'd be leaning one way or the other. Always after I put the ladder away or when straightening her risked knocking off lower ornaments. She knew this—I was sure.

An angel who looked like she'd hit the eggnog a little too hard had become a Christmas tradition. Much like my family emulating her composure and supposed drinking problem during my Christmas eve party. Each year, my siblings and their current mates or spouses and kids would descend on my house. By the end of the evening, I'd hear several versions of, "Your angel's tipsy again." Often, multiple times from the same person at various stages of inebriation. The angel fit right in. One big, happy family.

Two Christmases had come and gone since I last hosted a party—since the divorce. We'd all started new traditions. And alone, or with just Jason home, I didn't drink during the holidays. Not much at all, for that matter. Just didn't keep any in the house. Unlike some of my family, I learned that lesson. Unfortunately, a little late.

I glared at the angel before putting the ladder in the garage. She still had a chance to lean over. I had left the bottom of the tree for Jason to decorate. Not that he cared to. By ten years old, these modern kids were beyond Christmas traditions other than the presents. Why she chose this year to straighten up, I don't know. Only Jason and I would witness her sobriety, and he didn't care.

You see, it was my year to have Jason the week before Christmas. Sarah dropped him off promptly at four after his last day of school. I heard the car in the driveway, so pulled the drapes aside and peered out. True to habit, Sara gave a single stroke wave when she got back in the car. I returned the gesture, but waited for her to turn the car down the street before stepping out to help Jason carry in his bag and a couple colorful packages.

When we reached the front door, my phone was buzzing in my pocket. I set the boxes down inside and answered it. "Hey, Mom... Yeah, happy holidays... Your oven's dead?... Just a sec. Jason just got here and I'm helping him bring his stuff in... No, hang on... It's just my arms are full." I muted the phone and found Jason unpacking in his room. "Hey, is it cool if grandma and grandpa have dinner with us Christmas eve? Their oven died."

"Grandma and grandpa? Sure."

I put the phone back to my ear. "Okay, Mom. You say your oven's dead?... Sure... Jason and I'd love to have you... We can cook it all here."

That evening, I lit the tree and Jason finished decorating it. Well, he added a handful of ornaments and I filled it out. I usually played Christmas music while I decorated, but didn't press my luck with Jason. Better no music than him popping in his earbuds.

After clearing the empty boxes and putting the wrapped ones under the tree, I asked him, "Rudolph or Frosty first?"

"Whatever."

"We don't have to do either," I said. "I know you only watch these for my sake."

"No problem. Better than the tear-jerkers Mom watches."

"Does *she* make you watch those with her?"

"No, but I always have to bring her a box of tissues, so she doesn't have to leave the couch."

"I hate those shows," I said. "Supposedly new ones every year, but they're all the same."

I realized I said too much when Jason stared at me instead of his phone.

"Rudolph, then," I said.

Jason queued the movie while I popped popcorn and we settled on the couch. He fiddled with his phone while I watched the movie. About the time Mrs. Santa was forever damaging children's eating habits, Jason said, "Hey, Dad. Do you mind if Mom comes over Christmas eve?"

Jason understood the divorce. He didn't even try to reunite the family the first Christmas. Yet, I didn't grasp the question, or I did and didn't believe it. "Jason, you know we have separate lives now—"

"She asked, Dad."

"You better tell her about your grandma and grandpa..."

"I did."

To satisfy my disbelief, he raised his phone. Though I'd had a cell phone for as long as I could remember, I wasn't born with one in my hand and the speed of communication still baffled me. Which now, as my phone buzzed, could be my undoing. The display read, "George."

"Better hold off," I said to Jason, tipping my phone toward him. "It's Uncle George."

"Yeah, George... I thought you were... A tropical storm?... That sucks... Of course you can... Mom and Dad will be here... No. We have everything... See you then."

I grimaced at Jason. "Looks like Uncle George will be here, too. If your mom still wants to come, she's welcome. I'd like that. But I'd understand."

"She'll think about it," he said, showing his disappointment. Apparently, he shared the news while I was still on the phone.

My phone buzzed again. This time it showed "Cheryl." Just as Frosty was springing to life, my Christmas eve was keeling over dead. I should have guessed. My sister and her kids had planned on having dinner with our folks. I didn't want to answer it and frowned an apology at Jason. His hopes were being dashed along with mine.

"Hi, Cheryl," I said into the phone. "Yeah, they're coming here... ...I understand... ...Of course, you're welcome... So, five of you... And his mother... Of course, she can... So six... ...Seven... See you then... Yeah. Bye... mmBye."

"I'm sorry, Jason. I couldn't say 'no.' I've—"

"She'll come," he said.

"Mom?"

"Yeah. What can she bring?"

"Nothing. Herself," I rambled.

He waited for an answer. He knew his mom would insist on bringing something.

"An appetizer," I said. But thought, "Anything but booze."

He texted something on his phone.

"You don't have to watch the rest of this," I said.

Jason set a box of tissues on the side table before heading to his room. "Spoiler alert. Frosty's about to melt," he said.

Over my shoulder, I watched him leave, then took a tissue. Gazing up at the angel, I said, "I'm counting on you."

The lights on the tree winked off and back on. It might have been a power glitch or the water in my eyes or the twenty-year-old lights starting to fail. But I knew it was none of these.

About Christmas Angel

Original holiday stories are especially difficult because so many have been written and every plot seems cliché. If you enjoyed *Christmas Angel*, look for *Mother's Mincemeat: Home for the Holidays* in *Flashing Lights: Short and Weird Volume 2* (2024).

Prompt

What if the "Christmas Angel" at the top of my tree was an actual angel?

Inspiration

The inspiration for *Christmas Angel: Leaning Into Christmas* came from my Christmas tree decorating experience. The angel at the top of my tree is very much like the one in the story. To my eternal frustration, she always takes the drunken composure described in the story once I've finished decorating the tree and have put the ladder away. For the record, until recent years, my Christmas trees were usually eighteen to twenty feet tall. There are plenty of stories there, I assure you. The rest of the story was a gift from my overactive imagination.

Rainbow Catcher: Capture the Moment

PG: Mainstream, Portal, Sci-Fi, YA

Mesmerized by the brightly painted carnival attractions and flashing lights of all colors, Will gazed down the boardwalk. He stopped walking while Jim ran ahead. He was afraid of stepping in something gross when he wasn't looking, and of ruining his new All Stars—new to him, anyway. They were Jim's until a week ago.

"C'mon Will. Let's get in line for the coaster," yelled Jim.

Will ran to catch up with his older brother. Mother had allowed the tweens to go to the carnival only on the promise they'd stay together. Even then, it took a full night of pleading and promising to persuade her. And then, all morning to get an advance on their allowances. This time tomorrow, they'll be washing the Pinto. But that was tomorrow.

As they approached the rides and the crowd grew around them, they slowed their run to a fast walk. Jim's legs had grown what must have been three inches just over the summer. Now, they were so much longer, Will had to jog every other step to keep up. He felt the urge to hold Jim's hand, but that was childish. This was the year he would ride the coaster and he had to be big to do that. And he was. Jim measured him before they left the house.

"Hey Will. Look at this." Jim stopped in his tracks and Will almost ran into him. Jim was standing in front of a mirror that made him look short.

The one in front of Will made him look tall. They laughed and pointed at each other's reflections. "Don't you wish," said Jim.

"Yeah." But Will looked up at his brother standing next to him and thought, *No*. He liked having a big brother. One who had done everything first. Like riding the coaster.

Between the mirrors was an old coin-op fortune teller. Its lights flashed and its speaker crackled with a sound like thunder. Then, the ominous voice of the turbaned Zoltan called out, "Let me tell your fortune—" But it was drowned out by the roar of the coaster wheels and screams of the riders zipping by behind the boys.

"Let's hope you don't need that mirror to get on the coaster."

"Funny. I'm tall enough."

"I dunno. Maybe they raised the height limit. After what happened to that ten-year-old kid from Green Town last year..."

"There was no kid from Green Town last year." Jim was always saying things like that. It was probably something Dad would say. But now it was up to Jim to say these things. "You just want me to be as scared as you were your first time."

"I wasn't scared," said Jim. "I was *terrr-ri-fied*." He grabbed Will's hand and yanked him toward the painted wood clown marking the start of the coaster line. "Let's make sure."

"Same clown," said Will as they stopped in front of the faded wooden standee. Half the letters in "You must be taller than me" had chipped off, but the message was clear. And suddenly, Will wasn't so sure. He had insisted on wearing the All Stars, but they measured his height in the thick-soled "earth shoes" mom had bought him at Goodwill. He stood tall with his back to the clown.

Jim barked orders at Will with a horrible German accent like when they played "Hogan's Heroes." "Ten-hut. Heels on the ground. No cheating." Jim put his palm on Will's head and made noises with his mouth as he measured. "Good thing you got a pointy head," he said. "Let's go, LeBeau."

They rode the coaster three times in a row. First, sitting in a middle car, then in the last, then they waited forever for the front car. Will even kept his eyes open the whole way on the last ride. Except in the tunnel, but that didn't count since it was dark in there, anyway. They were in line for a fourth and final ride when it started to rain and the ride closed.

"Let's get lunch and figure out what to ride next," said Jim.

But everyone on the boardwalk must have had the same idea. The lines for food were longer than the one for the coaster had been. "By the time we get up there, the line will be short again," said Jim, showing wisdom beyond his years. "Let's check out the games."

The rare and amazing smell of greasy corn dogs made Will's mouth water. But he said, "Good idea," which he was always saying to Jim.

Jim bought midway tickets, just leaving enough money in his pocket for one lunch for them to share. Of course, Jim went straight to the baseball throw. He was the pitcher for their sand lot team and had a good arm, but the booth was crowded with older boys and their girlfriends. *Show-offs,* thought Will. *Next year, Jim will show you.*

Will grabbed Jim's arm and tugged him toward the next booth, where there was no line. The BB guns. They were both good shooters. And though it was hard to tell with soup cans for targets, Will might even be a little better than his older brother. "I challenge you to a duel," he said.

"You got it, hombre."

There were ducks floating by in a water trough and other birds and squirrels popping up from behind silhouettes of bushes and trees, each with a red, black, and white target painted on it. "What?" said Jim. "No soup cans?"

They laughed as Jim counted out the tickets. They hadn't noticed the odd, wiry man behind the counter until his long fingers reached for the tickets. Will looked at the bony hand, attached to an arm and a man who looked like he was made of wire. He handed them each a pair of glasses. "You have to wear these for safety," he said in a voice as creepy as his long fingers.

When Will put his pair on, the colored lights reflected off the scratches on the lenses. "Do we have to?" he complained. "I can barely see through these."

"Sorry," said the man. "It's the rules." He pointed toward a white sign with red lettering. Will couldn't read it through the smudged and scratched glasses, but he knew what it must say.

Will and Jim both spit-cleaned their lenses and tried them on again. Will's were a little better, but the targets were still obscured and he had to hold his head just so, to avoid the prism of lights. "Do you have any better glasses?" he asked.

"Believe me, those are my best," said the man.

Looking at the run-down booth, Will believed him.

"You can use your own if you'd like."

"Didn't bring any. Here," said Jim, tapping Will on the shoulder. "Try mine. They might be better." They swapped glasses, and Jim's were about the same. "You want those or swap back?" he offered.

"Seems like we're even."

"It's rigged," said Jim. "So, let's just see who does best."

"I'm sorry about the glasses, boys. I'll make you a deal. I'll guarantee our best prize for whoever wins the best of three."

Will was better at math and spoke first. "That would take all our tickets, Jim."

"Only if I don't waste you in the first two rounds."

"Sounds like the gauntlet has been thrown," said the man.

Will had heard the saying in a movie before, and now knew what it meant. "You are so gonna lose."

But Jim scored the highest with the first round of twenty-five BBs. Despite poor vision through the glasses, they both hit targets with most of their shots. Jim's were just worth more points.

"You're both very good shots," said the man. "Even with the crummy glasses."

After the first few shots in the second round, Will noticed when he held his head just right, the prism of colors highlighted the target and helped him line up the shot. It was obvious well before the last shot, but when Will hit his final target, he said, "Smoked you."

"No kidding," said Jim. "How'd you do that?"

"Wouldn't you like to know?" teased Will, but then he showed Jim what he was doing.

When Jim figured it out, he looked at the man. "Hey, these are trick glasses, aren't they?"

The man loaded the guns with new BBs. "I think you two are trick shooters."

This round, both boys hit their targets and tied. Will looked at Jim and then at the man. "What now?"

"You creamed me that second round," said Jim. "And you figured out the trick glasses. I think you won."

"I agree," said the man. "So you get the prize, Will."

It seemed odd the man called him by name, but Will figured he must have heard Jim say it.

"What is it?" the boys asked in unison. They hadn't even known what the prize was.

Jim elbowed Will. "It's probably that big pink rabbit."

"Better than a big pink rabbit," said the man. "Hard to believe, I know." From what seemed out of nowhere, a brass tube appeared in his hand. It must have been hidden beneath the counter. As the man pulled on the end, the tube extended, and a glass lens in its end reflected the sunlight.

"Looks like a spyglass," said Jim.

"Even better than a spyglass. It's a rainbow catcher." He held the tube out to Will. "Go ahead Will, it's yours. Look through it."

Will took it and put the end to his eye. He turned so he could point the tube at the top of the coaster hill. The links in the tow chain were rolling over the gear. "It is a spyglass." He handed it to Jim. "You can see the top of the coaster."

Jim took it and looked through it. "Hey, the coaster just went by. No one in it, but they're testing the track." He handed the spyglass back to Will. "Maybe we can do another ride, then get back in line for the coaster."

"What makes it a rainbow catcher?" Will asked the man.

"If you look through the glass at a rainbow and don't blink, you capture that picture in the rainbow catcher. Like a movie camera."

"Then what can you do with it?" asked Will.

"You can keep that picture forever or until you look at another rainbow and capture that one."

Jim laughed. "Sure. It's a spyglass, Will. Let's ride the Ferris wheel. There's never a line there until dark," he said nodding back toward the baseball throw. "And those dopes can kiss without their parents seeing."

Will held the rainbow catcher reverently between the man and him. "Thank you, sir."

"Yeah," said Jim. "Thanks. We had fun. And that *rainbow catcher* is a super prize." He gave the man an obvious wink. "Even if it is just a spyglass."

Before Jim could run off, Will asked, "What about lunch?"

"We want to be the first ones on the rides. Ferris wheel, Coaster, lunch. Deal?"

"Deal."

As the boys rounded the corner of the booth, Will saw the colors and lights of the Ferris wheel overwhelmed by a brilliant rainbow arch over its top. He grabbed Jim's arm and stopped at the entrance to the ride. "I got an idea. You ride the Ferris wheel and I'll wait for you down here."

"What's the fun in that?"

"I want to look at you through the spyglass when you're at the very top."

"I dunno, Will. We're supposed to stay together."

"I'll stand right over there where you can see me the whole time."

"It's not the same."

"Please." *I want to capture this day forever.*

"Okay, but you can't tell Mom I left you alone. It's not lying if you just don't say anything."

"I won't."

Jim hesitated, then said, "Stay right there where I can see you," as he ran toward the line.

"Don't forget to wave from the very top," yelled Will.

There was a moment when Will couldn't see Jim through the people standing in line, but there he was, sitting in a car, pointing at him, jerking his arm back and forth. Will couldn't hear him, but knew what he was saying. "Stay right there."

As each car loaded, the wheel rotated, Jim rose along its arc, getting closer to the top, closer to the rainbow. And with each ratchet of the wheel, Jim pointed at Will. "Stay right there."

When Jim reached the top, Will looked at him through the rainbow catcher. Jim stuck out his tongue, stuck his thumbs in his ears and wagged his fingers. Then, with a smile as big as the rainbow overhead, he waved at his little brother with both hands. Will watched without blinking until his eyes watered, then lowered the rainbow catcher and waved back with one hand, wiping his eyes with the other.

The Ferris wheel must have been loaded because it started to turn without stopping.

Flash! The sky between the tiniest cloud overhead and the hub of the Ferris wheel, the space between Will and Jim, ignited with a bolt of blue-white light. Crack! Will's eardrums burst and started ringing.

The Ferris wheel broke loose and rolled along the boardwalk. People scattered from its path, some falling under its crushing weight. Will chased after it, looking for Jim's car. Was it faded blue or green? The horrible crunching of the wheel and the screaming of the crowd rose above the ringing in Will's ears. Then the wheel rolled off the end of the boardwalk and into the shallow sea before stopping and toppling to the side with a great splash.

• • • • • • • • • •

Jim was never found. Among the many injured and several killed, there was no sign of the smiling twelve-year-old. After days of digging through the rubble, diving to the ocean bottom, and holding candle-light vigils, the rescuers gave up the search.

Though Will couldn't explain why, he convinced his mother they needed to talk to the man who ran the BB gun booth. But the carnival operators said they had retired the booth years before "due to liability concerns." Strangely, though, Will's description of the man fit the booth's attendant, who was no longer with the carnival. Like most carnies, his current whereabouts were unknown.

And though Will had promised Jim he wouldn't, he told their mother how they became separated.

On the brightest of days, when there was no possibility of a rainbow in sight, Will and their mother watched the mini-movie of Jim making faces and waving at Will. And they traveled the country, visiting every carnival, looking for the wiry man who might know how to free Jim from the rainbow catcher.

About Rainbow Catcher

Rainbow Catcher captures much of what I loved about science fiction when I was first introduced to the genre—the sense of wonder and mystery—the wide-eyed perspective of tweens looking for excitement in the mundane. And finding it. If you enjoyed *Rainbow Catcher*, look for the *Rainbow Catch and Release* right bookend, *Rainbow Redux: Reflection Rescue* in *Flashing Lights: Short and Weird Volume 2* (2024).

Prompt

What if a moment viewed through a kaleidoscope-like device was captured forever?

Inspiration

The kaleidoscope evolved into the rainbow catcher, which really works, and a boy captures his brother in it. The story that developed is an homage to Ray Bradbury's "Green Town" books, *Dandelion Wine* (which is possibly my all-time favorite book of all genres—and I could never do justice) and, more obviously, *Something Wicked This Way Comes*.

Yes, I wore hand-me-down shoes and even had a new pair of "earth shoes" (though the fad was ending, so they were heavily discounted). They made you feel as if you were always walking uphill, which might be great for the calf muscles, but is metaphorically depressing. Apparently, you can still buy them. Who knew?

Easter Egg

The brothers talk about a boy from Green Town and the coin-op oracle Zoltan are references to Bradbury's fantastic classics.

Dead Man's Hand: The Only Good Cheat is a Dead Cheat

PG: Ghosts, Historical, Humorous, Western

Joe eyed the three grim faces around the poker table as the player to his right flicked the cards to each with grubby fingers. *Grubby.* The player to Joe's left was the only one slick enough to cheat a deal and needed to be watched. *Slick.*

Joe was holding his own in the game. Up some. Down some when he needed to be. Staying in while studying the other players.

Grubby and Slick spread their hands. Their eyes darted from their cards to each other, always resting too long on the cowboy in the black hat across from Joe. The one sitting comfortably, back to the bar, cool as midnight in May. The one they called Pike. The one who mattered.

But Joe knew that before he accepted the offered chair. The seat the regulars opened for him wasn't by chance. The head man always sat directly across, flanked by drovers who steered winnings and an occasional friendly card his way.

Forever the outsider, Joe knew he faced a posse at the table. *Same one that'll run me out'a town.*

Still, Joe liked his odds. He'd be disappointed if it were any other way. He could almost smell their confidence over the cigar smoke, the sweat, and the caramel of the whiskey.

They didn't know Joe wasn't playing alone either. He raised his whiskey and tipped his glass before downing it, saluting his partner, Bill, who'd been shot in the back in a game like this.

Joe studied his cards as he spread them. Queen of hearts. His eyes rolled up to meet the all-too-friendly smile of the redhead at the bar. She winked as she thrust her chest forward, straining her corset, and crossed her black-laced, milky thighs. *Like whitefish wrestling in a net.*

King of hearts. *No surprise.* Joe had spotted him before the batwing doors closed on the dusty street behind him. He didn't need to, nor dared, look at the gentleman in the corner with the bola tie, its silver and turquoise aiglets and concho clasp accenting his brocade vest. And, no doubt, the matching derringer in that vest pocket.

Ace of hearts. The bullet. *The barkeep.* Joe couldn't help but smile. Not for the hand shaping up to be a royal flush. *Nothing wrong with a royal flush.* But this was a hand for listening, not winning. The smile was for all the times he'd seen a barkeep or shotgun with his sights on the owner's gal.

A pair of black eights. Joe glanced to his right then left at Grubby and Slick. Brothers. Not so obvious the way they were attired, but the hook nose and little eyes, the long neck. *Should'a known.*

This hand was shaping up to be as predictable as a tarot reading, which reminded him. It wasn't uncommon for a merchant's wife or mother to offer tarot or palm readings in a town this size. It was rare, though, for one to give him any notice. This one, a young wife or daughter, stepped out of the milliner's shop and gave him a knowing look while he hitched his horse. *Best steer clear of her.*

The game was dealer's choice. In a stud hand, Joe was quick to learn the other players, their tells, their tricks, their tactics. And in a game like this, when they secretly played with house money, their roles in the swindle. In draw, his cards alerted him to everyone in the room. All the players, at the table and not. Dealer's choice was the best of both worlds. He could win big, fast, but had to pace himself.

As Joe's bet went around the table, seen by all, he heard the squeak and thump, thump of the batwings behind him.

Joe held the eights.

"Three," he said, setting the hearts on the table.

With each card dealt, came the patter of women's shoes on the floorboards. The gal he figured for the tarot reader stepped behind Pike and rested her left hand on his shoulder. Even in the dim saloon, the diamond in her ring sparkled beneath Pike's ear.

Joe picked up the cards dealt him. *What'a we know about Pike?*

Jack of diamonds and a pair of black aces. A dead man's hand. *Time to go.*

Joe bet, then folded when Pike raised him. The brothers folded in turn as well.

"One more," said Joe, while Pike raked in the pot.

"Quittin' kinda quick," said Pike.

The diamond was off his shoulder and the tarot reader a step back without a sound.

"Whiskey, I meant." Joe raised his empty glass toward the queen of hearts at the bar. "Another whiskey?"

"You bet, honey," she said, winking at him again, before turning to the bartender.

Two beaus not enough?

Joe collected the cards and shuffled while he waited for the whiskey. Then he set them down and offered the empty glass for the full one.

No sooner was the fresh glass in his hand, its contents were pickling Pike's eyes and the table was in his lap. The brothers were stumbling over their chairs. The barkeep was raising a shotgun.

And Joe's Colt was at Queeny's throat.

As Joe backed through the batwings, Queeny pressed hard against his chest. Her heart pounded. "We're riding this horse together," he said, grabbing the reins. "That fine with you?"

He didn't wait for her answer before mounting and lifting her to the horse's rump behind him.

"Let's ride, handsome," she breathed in his ear.

And they did.

The men in the saloon hit the doors at once and, despite the weight behind them, the batwings didn't budge. Then they swung open and dumped the men on the boardwalk in a heap.

When Joe was clear of town, he sat his horse. "Sorry to leave you out here," he said.

"I needed some excitement," said Queeny, nibbling his ear before sliding to the ground.

When Joe sensed Bill catch up, he said, "I know. You were right. Should'a lit out when that tarot gal gawked at us."

About Dead Man's Hand

Dead Man's Hand is a bit atypical of the short story series—like many of the tales, it is a ghost story and hopefully humorous, but it's also a western. If you enjoyed *Dead Man's Hand*, look for *Flash in the Pan* in *Flashing Lights: Short and Weird Volume 2* (2024).

Prompt

What if a wild west gambler's dead partner still helps him cheat?

Inspiration

Since my early youth, I have been an avid card player. As a tween and teen, I especially enjoyed it when I was teamed up with my brother Robert against my mom and grandma or another sibling in a partners game. (Usually a trick-taking game or canasta). One of our favorite things to do was make up ways to pretend we were cheating. We knew exactly how the other played a hand and mopped the floor with our opponents, so we were perpetually accused of cheating. Why not let them believe we were? We'd say nonsense phrases like, "The daisies are growing on the roof," or tap on the table in fake code.

So, in developing the story, I thought about how a ghost partner would communicate with his buddy. It's all in the cards. Then, of course, how someone could see through their scheme. It looks like this time; the supernatural duo met their match.

Fall Colors: Death is Beautiful

PG-13: Horror/Suspense, Humorous, Mainstream, Mystery, Seasonal

Zoe and I had been watching the news for the best day to see the fall colors. After alarming alerts about climate change, contaminated food recalls, and government corruption, the one bright topic the local news reported on was the changing of the aspen. Timing the jaunt into the mountains to view the gold and orange and red flashes of the distinctive fluttering leaves is newsworthy because peak viewing is often a matter of days, not weeks. In Colorado, spring and fall are my favorite two weeks of the year.

The group from the botanic gardens is going on Saturday and Treasure the Trees, the group we usually go with, on Sunday. So, I was surprised when Zoe suggested we go alone midweek. Though I hadn't been to a Treasure the Trees meeting in at least a year, Zoe and I first met at a sit-in they organized. It was love at first sight. Later, I thought it might have been an effect of the wild mushrooms we ate, but we've been together ever since. And that's with eating only mushrooms I can buy at the grocery store.

Anyway, the aspen trip is a sort-of anniversary for us. So, we look forward to it. Sort of.

Zoe's suggestion alone was enough to convince me. With the log-jam of sightseers creeping through the winding canyons, weekend traffic is always a mess. Besides, the tree lovers are all *Zoe's* friends now. Sure, I still care about the environment, but I can't stand their grim faces, elongated with concern, when Zoe tells them about the many ways I've fallen off the wagon. And then my compulsory but feigned interest in the books and YouTube videos they recommend that will surely lift me back on board. Zoe calls me a poser, but I'm not the one whose driver's license says "Martha."

It will be refreshing to get back to nature and back to just the two of us. Well, back to nature anyway. I'm not sure we ever had the other. As much as I thought I wanted it.

So, we're going today, Tuesday, which is why I'm only now getting out of the shower. If nothing else, it felt good to ignore the six a.m. alarm and sleep in for an extra hour.

As I towel off, I hear her voice from somewhere in the house. "Do we need to get gas for that polluter of yours?"

"No. I filled up on the way home last night." I call back.

We'll take my Jeep Wrangler instead of her Prius. Not that we'll need four-wheel drive, but it's the mountains—you drive the Jeep. Besides, if the weather's nice enough, we can drop the top.

By the time I'm ready to go, Zoe has the picnic packed in the Jeep and is waiting for me. "Sorry," I say. "Didn't realize you were so eager to get going."

"You know it's my favorite drive of the year."

I pat the canvas top like it's a puppy. "Might be a bit cool, but up or down?"

Zoe looks up at the cloudless Colorado sky. "Down. I'll get a sweater."

I lower the top while she walks back into the house. "Do *that* with your stupid Prius," I mutter as I collapse the top. I look over my shoulder, and seeing no Zoe, I search for any real food in the picnic basket, really a reusable hemp shopping bag supposedly sewn by the homeless. If there were any chips, they'd be on top. I hope.

I don't see anything edible, except maybe the gluten-free bread. So I dig under the paper plates, napkins, plasticware... I feel the cold curve of a frozen water bottle, then pull out a gallon Ziploc of chopped vegetables, orange and green and white. I stuff it back down to the bottom of the bag and feel something stiff and straight and... it takes my mind a second to realize the sting of pain in my finger. I yank my hand out, holding our large chef's knife by the blade. Reflected sunrise flashes in my eyes as I examine it.

I transfer the knife to my other hand so I can inspect my cut finger. I'm suck-soothing my finger, metallic flavored blood oozing from the cut, when I notice Zoe standing in front of me staring.

"Did you cut yourself?" she asks.

I open my mouth only long enough for one word. "Yeah."

"Let me see it," she says, taking my injured hand in both of hers.

I let my finger slip from my mouth when she tugs on my hand. "It doesn't look too bad," she says, examining the cut. Little pearls of blood form along the pink line of the slit. She kisses it, then lets go.

"Give me that and go get a Band-Aid." She takes the knife from my hand.

"Nah, it's fine." I take a white napkin from the picnic bag, wrap my finger with it, and squeeze it like I'm doing a hand strength test for the doctor. "What were you thinking, putting that knife in there?"

"Why were you digging in the bag?"

"I wanted to make sure you remembered my salami and cheese."

"They're in the cooler, meat brain."

She hadn't answered my question. "What's the knife for?"

"I thought you might need it to murder same salami and cheese."

"It's all pre-sliced." *Like my finger*, I say in my head. "You should have wrapped the blade in something."

"I thought it was safe in the bottom of the bag. I knew it was down there, and you didn't need to get in the bag. How was I to know you didn't trust me to pack your... lunch?"

"It's not that I didn't trust you. I just figured you wouldn't want to touch it."

"Well, I didn't. That's why my veggies are in the bag. But I did it for you, anyway."

"Thanks." *Still shoulda wrapped the blade.*

"Let's get going," she says, wrapping the blade with another napkin.

"We don't need the knife," I say. "You already murdered your veggies."

"Funny."

Apparently not, I think.

"I already locked up and you've made us even later."

I made us late?

She slips the knife into the picnic bag. "Let's just get going," she says, jumping into the passenger seat.

It's silly to keep the knife in there. We haven't left the house. So what if it's locked up. But before I protest, I think, *No biggie. Besides, it might come in handy.*

I dab my finger with the clean side of the napkin. Just a tiny red spot on a field of white. *We're good.* The other side looks like a red Rorschach test. I give it a quarter turn. *An aspen tree,* I say in my mind to the dour doctor.

"Are you coming?"

"Sorry. Yeah. Just cleaning up my..." I finish in my head, *finger that you cut.* I look for a place to discard the napkin and grin at the open top of the picnic bag. But I wad it up and stuff it in my pocket.

"Sorry I made us late," I say, as we pull out of the driveway. *At least I got one "sorry" in early. Wait. That's two already.*

She turns her head toward me. "It's OK. We have all the time in the world." She smiles. "The whole day to ourselves," she adds.

I look ahead at the stop sign and start braking. There's something wrong with her lips, though, so I look back. There's a red smear on one side, but she doesn't wear lipstick. Nothing more than sunscreen. "You have something on your lips," I say.

She licks her lips from side to side, top then bottom. "Did I get it?"

My head swivels between the road and her smile. Kinda like it did our first few months together. *Kinda.* "Looks like you got it."

The drive to the hills isn't far, but long enough that a little music would shorten it. I turn on the stereo and my "My I'm Large" CD starts playing. I sing along under my breath, "Please let me be—"

"What is this?" Zoe asks.

"The Bobs," I say.

"Can't we just enjoy the ride without music?"

"Sure." I turn the stereo off, but the song continues in my head.

After several miles of nothing but the whoosh of the wind, Zoe says, "I was reading about aspens last night. It was so interesting that I read until I fell asleep on the couch."

"Yeah?" *So interesting you fell asleep*, I think. *Not sure that makes sense.*

"Did you know the largest single living organism on Mother Earth is an aspen forest in Pando, Utah?"

"I'd heard something like that. Didn't know if it was urban legend."

"It's true. Most aspen groves are just a few unique organisms."

"I know if you plant one in your yard, they'll pop up all over the place and you'll likely never get rid of them."

"Why would you get rid of them?"

"Not great if you're trying to keep a lawn."

She's quiet for a while. "Can you imagine if they could think?"

"What? Aspens?"

"Yeah. One of those big groves of the same being."

"I hadn't thought about it," I say. All I can think about now is how Zoe got on this weird subject and were any wild mushrooms involved.

We get out of the city, leaving its awful sewer-smoke smells and nuisance noises behind. I inhale the pine scent—the kind that doesn't come from a chemical in a bottle. I listen for birds or bugs—anything but humans and their machines. Under the high whistle of air rushing over the windshield, I hear a low humming-like noise, rising and falling. The stereo's still off. The Jeep's running fine. I realize it's coming from the passenger seat. I look over at Zoe, who's watching the roadside over her half-door.

"You OK?" I ask.

She startles and turns toward me. "Yeah. Fine. Why?"

"I thought I heard you moaning."

"Oh. I didn't notice. Just a little carsick, I think."

"Want me to pull over for a bit?"

"No. I'm fine. We're almost there."

"All right. Let me know, though."

"There are small clusters of aspens already. I never noticed them along here before." She turns her head to watch the hillside rising beside us.

"Me neither," I say, spotting a clump of the trees ahead. Most of their leaves are still green at this low elevation. As we pass the aspens, I look at Zoe, focusing my ears on her.

She turns quickly to look back at me. "What?"

"Just making sure you're OK."

She gives me a flat smile and says, "So thoughtful." Then she turns back to her sightseeing.

A car pulls out from a side road ahead. There's plenty of room, but as we close the distance to it, I notice a bumper sticker, actually on its bumper. Not like the collection wallpapering the entire back of Zoe's Prius. The sticker reads, "HONK If you love me."

So, I honk, if for no other reason than to break the silence in the Jeep. Then I worry the driver will think I was honking because they pulled in ahead. I wave... I hear a double "beep-beep" and see a hand jutting through the driver's window, waving. I wave again over the top of the windshield.

Zoe's voice hits me from the side. "What are you doing?"

"Their bumper sticker says, 'Honk, if you love me.'"

"And you love the person in that car?"

"No. I love you, Zoe."

She stares at me.

"I honked because I love *you*, Zoe."

I don't get the response I would have, just a few years ago. "So you waved at *them*?"

"I was afraid..." Now, I'm afraid I can't win the argument that's about to erupt from the moaning mountain. "Never mind. I honked because I love you."

And now I get the response I've learned to expect. "You must be suffering from meat brain again. Did you see their other sticker?"

I look at the rear bumper, and read along as Zoe recites it to me. "Smith for Governor."

"What kind of creep has a 'Smith for Governor' sticker on their car?"

"Don't *you* have a Smith—"

She cuts me off. "That was before the fascist retweet. I covered it over when I voted to recall the creep."

"I hadn't noticed." *How could I?* I thought. *One statement among many. I could never keep up.* "So Smith was recalled?"

"No. Because meat brains like you didn't vote."

"I'm sorry." *That's three already.* "I think I was on a business trip, but should have made arrangements."

"You didn't even know who our governor is. Just now."

"You're right. I'm sorry." *That one doesn't count as four since it's the same argument.* "Just a lot on my mind lately."

"Yeah. Meat."

Stepped into that one. Meat and cheese on wheat bread, I think defiantly. After a quiet but not peaceful moment, I ask, "Can we just enjoy the scenic drive?"

"That's what I'm trying to do."

I foresee another "sorry" in my future before this will blow over, but I'll save it for when we get to our picnic spot. Let the scenic drive work its calming magic. It proves to be a wise move when we come around a bend and get our first look at why we come here. The splashes of gold, orange, and red of the aspen groves growing in clumps among the dark green pines coax an "Ooh" from her.

As we approach the intersection where our route leaves the highway, I let off the gas to slow down.

"Here's our turn," she says.

I let the backseat driving go without comment. At least she's talking to me. And not moaning at the trees—whatever that was.

I turn the Jeep onto the dirt road that winds up the mountain. Dark pines crowd the roadside. The road is well maintained, but there's something special about driving a Jeep with dirt under the tires. The thrill of escaping civilization. I can sense that Zoe feels it, too. We smile at each other. Another turn onto a smaller, steeper road and we're climbing to the picnic spot.

As we pull into the parking lot, I hit the brakes just a little harder than necessary to hear the grind of the gravel as the tires scrape over it. When I kill the engine, I'm ready to apologize for the sudden stop, but the complaint doesn't come.

We hop out and walk to the overlook without bothering with the picnic stuff in the back. Our long drive is rewarded with vast swaths of bright colors where autumn sunsets have precipitated on the aspen leaves.

"Beautiful," says Zoe.

I inhale the fresh air deep into my lungs. "Yeah. Beautiful."

With the noise of the engine and the wind fading from my ears, I hear the rustling of the leaves in the breeze and the trickle of the nearby creek. I reach my arm around Zoe and she puts hers around me, enjoying the sight and sound of the valley together.

I don't want to say anything... because I'm always the one who spoils the mood... but my stomach is growling. "Shall we set the picnic and have a bite?"

"Sure," is all she says, but I hear the disappointment in her tone.

We turn to walk back to the Jeep and she reaches her hand in front of me. "Keys. I'll drive home."

I had already stuffed them in my jeans pocket, so I slip a couple fingers in and feel the bloody napkin. "Wrong pocket," I say, stuffing the napkin deeper before taking my fingers out. I try the other pocket and dig out the keys, then hand them over as we get to the Jeep.

We gather everything for the picnic in our four hands and I follow Zoe into a small clearing, surrounded by aspen, except a gap with a valley view. We set everything down and pause the picnic again to enjoy the view arm-in-arm.

Suddenly, my spine freezes. Not just a chill. Not an early winter fragment blown across my back. More like an icicle displacing my spinal cord, relaying cold across the synapses throughout my nervous system.

Then the feeling evaporates as quickly as it had formed. Zoe's arm-grip around my waist loosens as I relax mine on her. *Did she feel it, too?* I break the silence, suggesting we set our picnic more in the open.

"What's wrong with in here?" asks Zoe.

I glance around at the circle of aspen and then at Zoe. "It'll be warmer in the meadow."

She pinches the collar of her pullover. "I'm warm enough."

"It's kinda gloomy in here," I say.

"Gloomy?" She looks around. "It's beautiful."

"Yeah. I don't know what I was thinking."

I start to spread the worn, red-and-white-checked tablecloth on the ground and Zoe stops me.

"Let me clear the leaves away," she says, raking the fallen leaves with her fingers.

"They're just leaves. They're beautiful when they fall," I say. "After a night or two on the ground, they're just ugly old leaves. Crunch under your feet like potato chips."

But the look she gives me is enough to make me wait, resting each hand in the other armpit, the cloth draped down my body in red and white checks. "What's all this worry over a bunch of dead leaves?" I ask as she wipes her soiled fingers on her jeans.

"They're the fallen children of the trees," she says.

"Now, who's being gloomy?" I ask. "Sorry," I blurt out before she can respond. And *that* is the last sorry from me. *I'm sick of being sorry.* "Respect is good," I say. I even brush a few leaves she missed to the side as I spread the cloth over the ground.

We sit quietly as we eat—"quietly" meaning "without talking." Even positioned so she doesn't have to look at my sacrilegious sandwich, I hear her munching her raw vegetables. I wish I had some chips to match her crunching. *Chips are vegetables, too. Vinegar and salt, maybe.*

I gaze down the valley, thinking about potato chips. There's a patch of barbeque and another of Sriracha, all surrounded by traditional. Without thinking, I pick up a leaf and strip the blades away, leaving only the spine. It's an odd, old habit. I flick the spine down the hillside and pick up another.

Zoe's voice comes from behind me. "Let them rest in peace."

I realize what I'm doing and drop the leaf onto my jeans, then quickly brush it off into the pile along the edge of the cloth. I turn my head to look at her and say, "Sorr..."

She's holding the chef's knife like a gladiator, shaking it in my face with each word as she repeats, "Let them rest in peace." The blade flashes reflected light into my eyes.

I jerk my hands up between us, palms toward her in surrender. "Ok. Ok. I didn't realize what I was doing." Worse, I didn't notice what she was doing. *What the...*

"That excuse doesn't work anymore. Not when you sit here and eat a poor animal."

"Sorr—"

"And don't say you're sorry. I *hate* that. I know how sorry you are." She switches the knife to a Norman Bates hold. "Let's see how beautiful you can be," she says, teeth bared, eyes wide.

Surely, she won't—

Zoe drives the knife deep into my chest. I grab her arm to stop the second plunge, pull myself to my feet, and knock her to the ground. I stagger toward the Jeep, reaching in my pocket for the keys, but only pull out bits of bloodied napkin. *She took the keys,* I remember.

It doesn't matter, though. She's on me from behind. I look down as I fall to my knees and see the shiny tip of the blade vanish into my chest, replaced by a red spot blossoming on my white shirt. I turn at my waist to see where that came from and begin to fall over. Not quickly enough, though, because she body slams me to the ground. I lie there, sprawled, twitching... *fluttering?*

She stands over me and crashes the knife through my skull with super-Zoe force.

As my vision fades, she asks of the grove, "Isn't he beautiful?"

The trees nod in the chill autumn breeze, their beautiful children falling in colorful flutters around me.

About Fall Colors

Fall Colors is more than a bit atypical of the collection—it is the only horror story and the most satirical. An earlier edition is also from a time (1987) when we could laugh at ourselves, so the satire is less politically correct in 2023.

Prompt

What if the largest organism on planet Earth is not only sentient, but sinister? And could speak telepathically to select humans?

Inspiration

For those unaware, the largest living single organism on Earth (which, as far as we know, means in the universe) is an aspen grove near Pando, Utah. I thought the aspen might enjoy watching the watchers succumb to a deadly fall. This is especially troubling to me since I live in the middle of an aspen grove.

The original (1985) version of the flash fiction story was just that horrific tale. I later merged it with a troubled but humorous relationship based on the satirical song "Please Let Me Be Your Third World Country" by the San Francisco-based (and one of my favorites) acappella/comedy group, The Bobs. If you are unfamiliar with the song, give it a listen on their website or YouTube.

Important Note: The sentiments expressed by the character telling the story or by Zoe are not my own, nor those of The Bobs. It is satire.

Very Important Note: No aspen trees were injured in the writing of this story.

Easter Egg

Zoe suggests going for a Band-Aid, which was certainly an event she would have "gone for."

You're Fired: Combustion Claim

PG: Humorous, Mainstream, Sci-Fi

We weren't paying on this policy, was what Carson was telling me in so many words. His face was red, a purple vein pulsed on his forehead, and he was out of breath from yelling for the last ten minutes. Carson was always calm, professional, as he walked about the office, but his forecast illustrations went nonlinear when someone filed a claim that smelled bogus, and when the coverage was eight figures, he went off the chart.

This claim stunk so bad even I could smell it, so I wasn't surprised when he had closed the door behind me after pointing to his guest chair. When the door closed, the lid came off his aggression. As manager for our premium policies, I was the one who usually witnessed his transformation. It was never a personal attack, or at least rarely, but I always left his office with my tail between my legs after one of these sessions. It was perfectly natural for him to scream at me like this; my reason for keeping my resume current. For the day I lost control and screamed back.

"Spontaneous combustion?" he screamed.

"Spontaneous internal human combustion," I said, holding the report between us as if I was reading from it. I had already read the report so I could recite it from memory if needed, but the separation was comforting.

"Come on, Terry," he said.

I thought he might be complaining about me using the file as a firewall—my reputation for having a photographic memory robbed me of the standard office defenses, like pretend-reading a report to buy time or to hide behind it. But his mind was on this case. When I peeked around the file, he wasn't even looking at me. I probably could leave the room and he'd still be screaming at the empty chair.

"Don't make it sound so scientific," he continued. "You know this is bogus. I'm not paying a cent and that policy holder will pay for my inconvenience."

I wasn't to take his lambast personally, but *he* wasn't paying. *He* wasn't due reimbursement for being inconvenienced. *He* was taking this personally.

"Who's the beneficiary?"

"The widow is sole benny."

"You're going out there tonight. Shouldn't take long to prove this is fraud."

At least he was giving orders now. I'd be out of here soon. I stood up and glanced back through the glass wall behind me. Fortunately, the office was dead this morning and only Johnson and Kamil were there to witness my lashing. I wish he would at least turn the blinds when he drags me in here. Next time I'll do it before I sit down.

"I want to hear from you by end-of-day Monday. How we aren't paying."

Take all weekend if you need it. "Yes, sir." To have anything by Monday was impossible, but Carson knew it. I wouldn't get a start on the investigation until tomorrow, Thursday. He just wanted to know he wasn't paying by Monday.

Carson was looking at papers on his desk, a different case, or maybe a takeout menu. "Stay the weekend, if you want. Might be a nice little vacation."

He knew I'd have to work on it. "Sure. Thanks."

I started toward the door. It's a shame that Carson's becoming personable was the signal to leave.

"I'll get right on it," I said, opening the door.

"See you Monday," he said.

"End of day."

It was end-of-day Monday when I entered Carson's office again. I reached to turn the blinds, but Johnson and Kamil threw their hands up like I was spoiling their fun. I left them open. Might be best to have witnesses.

"Sit down," said Carson, after my butt was already in his guest chair. He didn't look up from his desk until I set my laptop on it.

"Tell me how you got us out of paying this bogus claim."

"That's where it gets complicated."

"Complicated, my... What did the beneficiary, the widow, have to say?"

"She wasn't available for comment, but I have her public statement and the police report."

"She grieving in solitude?"

"Sailing in the Bahamas."

"That doesn't look suspicious?"

"How it looks is not the issue. The facts are."

"Tell me the facts, then."

"Our insured checked into a clinic for a polysomnogram. A PSG. You know, the kind of study they do to see if you need a CPAP."

"I know the kind of study. I've done one."

"Great. You're familiar. I'll walk you through the incident. We have his car in the parking lot, video of him checking in, video of him during the study, no video of him leaving the room or the building. We have his DNA on a tongue depressor. There's no doubt it was him."

"DNA from the corpse?"

"No DNA from the corpse. None. Not his, not no one's."

"Assuming it was him, then, what happened?" He glared at me, aggravated he had to give the first inch.

"We have the monitoring logs of the sleep study. Electrocardiography, pulse oximetry, respiratory effort, CO2 levels, continuous sound and video recording. This guy was wired up. We even have something called penile luminescence." So, I made that one up. Carson looked down at his desk, feigning distraction. *Thought so.*

"So, he was wired up. What happened?"

"The meters banged their needles against the pegs. Core body temperature went through the ceiling. The guy lit up like a safety flare. With a flash and a 'whomp,' the room filled with smoke. Then the fire sprinkler triggered. When the spray knocked down the smoke, all that remained on the bed was a black silhouette on the soaking wet white sheets."

Carson's face was red from the top of his bald head to below the collar of his white twill shirt.

"The whole thing was over in a flash, you might say." That got the vein throbbing. "We have the video if you'd like to watch. It's enlightening." I started it playing on my laptop, then turned it for Carson to watch.

He watched, mesmerized. "That's crazy."

I heard the video loop from the beginning. He kept watching, but asked, "What did this guy do?"

"Recently retired."

"From?"

He had to ask. "He was an entertainer of sorts."

Carson knew when I was vague, I was dodging. "What sort?"

"An illusionist."

"You're kidding."

I hoped Carson wouldn't ask the name...

"What was his stage name? The name of his show?"

"Immolation Man."

"Now you're messing with me."

"I'm afraid not."

"So, you're telling me that we have to pay?!"

"You issued the wire this morning." I pointed at the laptop.

"I what... You're..."

I always thought smoke coming out of someone's ears was just an expression, but I could see it, smell it.

"Fired?"

Carson started to glow. Having watched the polysomnography video a hundred times, I knew to get back, toppling my chair, tripping over myself. Through the office window, I saw Kamil's stunned face before the reflected flash blinded me.

I was soaked from the sprinkler system before I could get up from the floor. Fortunately, the ruined laptop was the company's. Mine was already packed for the Bahama cruise.

About You're Fired

From the original concept of the story, the insurance claim just had to become more preposterous (if possible). In this very short story, I leave the details and mechanics of the potential fraud to your imagination.

Prompt

What if a life insurance claim is for a victim of spontaneous internal human combustion?

Inspiration

I conceived the story prompt way back in 1996 and even started writing a mystery novel or novella based on the concept. At some point, I realized there wasn't enough flash there for a longer mystery and let the case go cold. Then, when considering stories for this series, it was an obvious, flashy addition.

My inspiration was to write a bombastic story that was pure fun. I had fun writing it and hope you did reading it.

Eccentric Orbit: Fragile Cargo

PG: Aliens, Humorous, Mainstream, Sci-Fi

Right Bookend: Abduction Coordinator

Human specimens in the cargo hold can't see me through the mirrored glass, but it still creeps me out when one faces me, eyes focused on their reflection. My first time at the inspection window, I self-consciously touched my face where the captive's stare penetrated the barrier, feeling for a blemish or bit of fuzz or food stuck there that caught her attention.

The sensation was odd enough, but what really bothered me, what caused me to look away, was the breach of privacy. I imagine some people might get a voyeuristic thrill watching some unsuspecting person inspect their teeth for a bit of granola the tongue couldn't dislodge or their nose for the source of a distracting tickle.

Not me. For starters, I had been on the other side of that glass—where tonight's harvest now mills about in wonder and delirium. The memory of trying to reorient myself after the blinding, ear-splitting flash-bang of the abduction, feeling helpless and alone, is visceral. Each person in the hold, including myself when I was there, should be clearly marked "Fragile."

Since my promotion to this side of the glass, I've asked if the flash-bang, really more of a "pop-pop-pop," is absolutely necessary. The captors are looking into it, which I assume means nothing will change, just like any tech support request on terra firma. I think the painfully disorienting flash-bang is purely a means to make clear to the captives, with absolute certainty, "We are in control."

In time, the captives will introduce themselves, but unsettled by the transfer, they still eye each other with suspicion. Except two. Some always recover from the transfer more quickly than others. Completely unaffected, the video gamer has already discovered the beer tap and is testing its potability. Also of this haul, the stargazer is glued to the porthole view of the galaxy beyond Earth's atmospheric distortion. Since the blue marble is always in view, I assume the ship orbits Earth at a distance beyond detection.

At three in the morning, their local time, those two are just getting started, but the others would normally be asleep. On an average day, the rockhound would probably be about to wake up and eat a pre-packaged but sensible breakfast. The germaphobe would be trying to sleep, despite nightmares of giant germs induced by a poor diet and the sweat-sticky, plastic-wrapped mattress. And the lady from the grocery store... I don't know.

How she got caught in my field is a mystery—a grocery cart collision isn't ample cause. But "Grocery Cart," which is how I refer to her, doesn't strike me as a night owl. Right now, she's checking the purple bags under her eyes on the other side of the mirror, drawing the skin down with the pad of her finger, grimacing with fatigue or concern or both. As with others who face the mirror, my intrusion on her self-examination compels me to look away.

Yet I must watch. Not because it's enjoyable, but it's my job. At least, I view it as an important aspect of my job. When I agreed to collect specimens, I invoked my business law degree and argued for the right to audit the process, to ensure the safety of the fragile cargo. The contractual clause didn't come easy. Any clause requiring disclosure of the purpose of the abductions was summarily rejected. But the audit clause stuck when I posed the two as an either-or decision.

Before you think there is a moral bone in my body, let me be clear. This ethics crisis came after I negotiated a hefty payment. What's worse, like my summer jobs in college hanging sheetrock, I get paid by the piece. By the specimen. By the abducted human. A bounty, if you will.

It's true that I'm a sell-out, but I'm not cruel or an accomplice to destructive experimentation or torture or murder or worse—I'm sure that if I put my mind to it, I could imagine worse. The abductors were at this game long before I got involved. I spent three weeks in that cargo hold and I survived and am no worse for wear.

And... I got a job out of it. One I'm not proud of, but I'm not bothered by it either—something I remind myself regularly. I was less proud and more bothered by hanging sheetrock. Not that there's anything wrong with rocking and taping, it's a trick skill—I just sucked at it. What I don't suck at is collecting odd human specimens. I'm a natural.

...And my mind roamed while inspecting last night's haul through the window. I tend to ramble, which is why, other than negotiating my current contract, that business law degree didn't pan out so well.

Let me back up to the beginning.

Six years ago, I was abducted by... Aliens? A rogue science project? A secret government program? Future humans? An AI? I didn't know then and as yet still don't, but here are some details I have noticed.

The areas of the ship I have accessed on both sides of the one-way mirror are configured for humans. My test for this was to request the use of the lavatory, which was surprising only by how unremarkable it was. A stool with an upright tank (1.6 gallon flush) and a wall-mounted hand sink with a mirror over it. For obvious reasons, I did not look in the mirror. Despite the sudden tickle in my right nostril.

So unremarkable a bathroom it was, in fact, that I had never noticed that door off the corridor in my many walks from the teleporter to the viewing room and back. The door with "LAVATORY" emblazoned on it, that since then I cannot not notice. Maybe I had been unobservant before. Or maybe if I had asked for "les toilettes" the sparse white room would have a bidet instead of a tissue roll—mounted the wrong direction, I might add. Until I fixed it. While this "test" may sound like a bit of cleverness on my part, it was really just the result of a poorly timed teleport to the ship. Yeah, enough on that.

Though, based on the apparent size of the saucer when I have seen it overhead at the pickup zone, I have only visited a small fraction of the ship's interior. All of which looks suspiciously like the original *Star Trek* set. I have not asked to see the bridge, but I can imagine what it and the lift that would take me there look like. They would be absent the Star Trek crew and any lifeforms, though, I'm certain, not even a brain in a bottle. After six years of interacting only via voice and wire transaction, I know I will never see the abductors.

What I have seen of the ship, though, may be instructive or may be illusory. The human cargo area has individual sleeping quarters and commons areas which change function and amenities depending on the resident specimens. According to my strict advisement, nothing with screens ever appears in the bay—no TVs, game consoles, computers, nothing. And no books either. As much as I enjoy reading, it is a solitary activity that would destroy the subtle interrogations.

The time between when I identify the last of the specimens for a new haul and when they are teleported onto the ship may only be a few hours, but the amenities always fit the group's needs.

Features like a CrossFit gym and wine bar have come and gone. Permanent fixtures are a multi-purpose area with a perpetual hot and cold buffet and beer tap along one wall and shelves loaded with an assortment of board games and puzzles along another. The captors might have borrowed the floor plan from a cruise ship set for an IT or gamer convention.

My side of the mirror is less interesting. The teleportation room, the viewing room where I am now, and the short corridor connecting them are sterile and nondescript, but are also designed for humans. If I'd been smart during negotiations, I would have a buffet on this side. I assumed there would at least be snacks on the flight. Pretzels? My mouth waters as I eye the buffet on the other side of the mirror. Man, I miss those crab rangoons. Maybe I can get the recipe.

As I said, I have never met the abductors—I have only communicated with an omnipresent voice that sounds suspiciously like the *Lost in Space* robot, the 1960s version, but without the clever wordplay. I didn't know there was a remake until I searched YouTube for clips to compare the voice. I could have figured there was one, since Hollywood only makes remakes. And no, discovering the new series did not result in a YouTube rabbit hole. I watched the entire first season of the original, of course, to make certain the voice was right.

Combined with the *Star Trek* motif, the setting may indicate how long this abduction project has been active.

The voice comes from hidden speakers or some other technology unknown to me. In a spaceship that defies physics and teleports living humans back and forth to Earth, the means of producing surround sound audio is trivial. And yet, when I hear the voice, I always look in wonder for its source.

Back to my abduction. I had just moved to a new town, not really a city, and hadn't made any friends yet—I made no friends in the last place either, but am certain I would have, eventually. I attract a lot of human interaction, which I'll explain in a minute, but most of them bounce off. Anyway, I always try to live close to a wilderness area where I can hike, ride my mountain bike, and apparently, get abducted with no witnesses.

The birds were singing, the breeze blowing, and the sun setting as I hiked back toward my car. When the birds stopped tweeting, I thought they were just flitting off to bed. But the sudden silence should have alerted me. It wasn't quite dark yet, but an illuminated, shadowless circle around me became obvious, so I looked straight up. Straight into a painfully bright light emanating from a saucer that all turned into blue-green dots as my corneas conceded to the overwhelming flash. That's when the "pop-pop-pop" blasted my eardrums.

When I removed my hands from my ears and opened my eyes, I was standing in the middle of the common room—the one beyond the mirror—about where the gamer and rockhound are standing now, enthusiastically talking at each other. The conversation appears cordial, and each is nodding like they are listening, but neither hears a word from the other. It's not like there's a cone of silence around them, they just don't listen.

They talk. And talk. And that is what the captors want—captives who can talk endlessly on a topic without ever asking a question.

Which is exactly what I told the omniscient voice when it was interrogating me in that room.

Shortly after gaining my wits and verifying that I had all my clothes and my keys, everything but my electronics, I heard the voice for the first time. "You are not in danger."

I expected a "Will Robinson," but it continued with, "Please. Make yourself at home. You will not be harmed. Just a few questions. Then you can go."

Go where? When? I thought, looking at my wrist for the time and seeing only the tan line around my missing Fitbit.

As promised, I was not harmed, and as advised, I made myself at home. Right before my abduction, I was thinking about what I would get to eat on the way home. I'm always starving at the end of my hike, and an all-you-can-eat Chinese buffet had crossed my mind. Then I smelled the crab rangoons.

Where their introduction went awry was in the definition of "a few" questions. The voice asked me questions while I ate, while I lounged afterward, and as the food coma hit—questions about anything and everything from particle physics to fashion trends. The voice interrogated me over several days. Though respectful of some personal time, I was the lone captive, so had the captor's undivided attention.

My question of "Go where?" became pressing. Even if they released me where they found me, my car would have been towed. The voice assured me that my phone would be fully charged when it was returned to me so I could call for a ride home. I didn't ask if my wallet would be recharged as well for the cost of an Uber. Remember, I had no friends who would pick me up. Or would miss me, which got me thinking.

When I awoke on day four, after a plate of biscuits and gravy with two glistening sausage patties between the fluffy bread and the gray goo, I took the lead on the interrogation. My first question, of course, "Why me?" followed by, "Why are you asking me all these questions about topics I don't know?" and others, leading to "Why don't you ask the experts?"

"We tried that," said the voice. "We invited prominent scientists and academics in all fields."

Apparently, I had confused my "invitation" with a sudden and violent abduction, but I didn't quibble. I was in charge now, and the voice was answering me casually, candidly, and in complete sentences—even taking some of my advice. "And what happened?" I asked.

Majel Barrett's normal, soothing voice emanated from nowhere in the room—using her voice was the first bit of my advice the captors accepted. For a sample, I had directed them to an mp3 file on my phone, which I knew they had. Yes, I use it as a ringtone. OK?

Almost immediately, the voice changed to hers—not just the tone, but the cadence, clarity, intelligence... you get the idea. More than what they could reasonably get from my ring tone. Hopefully, they didn't sample it from YouTube, or their need for captives to interrogate along with my quickly developing plan could go bust.

Majel's voice said, "They withheld information they knew, concerned about something called attribution. Then they talked endlessly and authoritatively about topics in which they were not experts—to be blunt, completely ignorant."

"Go figure," I said. I knew the type all too well. I'd had those profs, seen those talking heads on the news.

"Also, they were missed during their visit with us."

"Not so much missed," I jested, "as their absence was noticed."

Majel actually chuckled. "No doubt," she said.

I let the use of "visit" for "incarceration" go without challenge. We were getting somewhere as I worked my angle. I opened the negotiation by returning to my original question, which had been hand-waved away. Can a bodiless voice hand-wave? "So, why me?" I asked.

"We discovered average people are more willing to answer questions about what they know and admit ignorance about what they don't."

Just as I suspected. "So, you resorted to a shotgun approach." As soon as the idiom left my mouth, my mind raced through possible weapons the captors might have and might use on me if I became too annoying. More annoying than a bunch of scientists and academics would be a stretch, even for me, but no one would miss me. They certainly knew that. I had invited them to scan my phone.

The tension grew as the pregnant pause gestated.

"You might call it that," she finally said. "Do you have a better idea?"

Whew. *As a matter of fact...* "What if I could bring you experts who would spill the beans on everything they know without you even having to ask one question?"

"That would be valuable," she said, coyly acknowledging she was completely onto my ploy.

"And they would not be missed—their absence would not be noticed."

"Go on."

I explained how I could assemble a collection of various experts at their request, recommended changes to their program, and negotiated my fee. In addition to Majel Barrett's voice, abductions en masse to limit the disruptive teleportation events and exposure to discovery, simply monitoring the captives' conversations rather than individual interrogations, and the wall of board games... all my ideas.

Majel's team—I assume there is a team of captors and Majel is just the emissary—executed the transition with frightening ease while I slept. We agreed I would inspect the setup, which I did when I awoke.

The cargo hold was reconfigured for multiple concurrent captives, the white tile and rigid chair in the interrogation room were replaced with comfortable carpet squares for meditation, prayer, or yoga, and the board games I had recommended were shelved and ready to play. As negotiated, Majel let me unbox, punch, bag, and sleeve the components of a couple of the games. There's nothing like it. Popping bubble wrap isn't even a close second.

Back in the now. It's time to explain how I assemble these experts. I'm what my friend George calls a freak magnet. I attract self-trained experts, fans, fanatics, freaks everywhere I go. They want nothing more than to talk about their one passion with anyone who will listen, anyone who is too considerate to run away. Me.

A free meal and free beer open them up like marigolds in May. Other than the occasional chef special, the captors didn't need to change the standard buffet items when switching from scientists to freaks. But the beer tap was installed on my insistence—that alone might have fixed their problem with the scientists and academics, but they wouldn't need me for that plan. So, I left that unsaid.

As I view the room now, Grocery Cart is taste-testing the buffet, one small dollop of each item. Maybe she's a chef or a health inspector. Or a food critic, who isn't these days. Hopefully, she doesn't pan the buffet on Yelp.

While the others are in full chat mode, she has yet to interact with any of her fellow captives. More hopefully, she doesn't get sent back without being useful. All money transfers to my offshore account are irreversible, but the return policy on a rejected captive is a fifty percent reduction from my fee for the next captive.

To avoid conflict or damage to the conversational mood, the occasional belligerent or unhelpful captive is released back into the wild immediately. Others are released as a group once their collective value has diminished. Abductions are amazingly easily concealed because the freak specimens are viewed as crackpots and aren't taken seriously—same as the scientists.

The greatest concern is one of population. Remote areas where the flashing lights and noises associated with the transfer are lower risk but have a limited supply of freaks. Urban areas where there is an abundant supply are also where the transfer is most likely to be noticed. Difficulty keeping the operation concealed is why I have to move often or take extended vacations to scout new locations, gravitating who I can elsewhere. Areas like the Colorado Front Range and Pacific Northwest where major urban centers with a high freak ratio are proximate to unpopulated wilderness are prime locations. And how I have managed to stay put for three years now.

When the abductors release a group, I'm alerted via a text message, usually accompanied by an order for a new shipment. As you might guess, the sender is "MB"—one of only three named contacts in my phone that aren't business names.

The message is always simple, something like, "More, please." Unless the abduction site changes, anything more specific isn't helpful since I can't predict what type of specialists I will attract or how many. I aim for three to five and sweep active public locations until I meet the quota. Then I text back with something equally brief, like, "Tonight," and deliver the order.

To say that I deliver the captives to the abduction site is a bit of a stretch. I just go there and they are drawn to me or to a beacon set by the captors—I'm not really sure how it works. I've had to pick up captives twice, ones who "never learned how to drive," and sent an

Uber once to a captive without a car or phone. Otherwise it's pretty simple.

Before you get worked up, thinking I'm aiding the abduction of children, it doesn't happen. Young people, for some that can be as old as thirtyish, talk like they are experts on everything, which means they are experts in nothing. It takes years of dedication to become a freak-level specialist. Similarly, you might think it would be easier for me to trawl online, but my freak magnetation doesn't work remotely. Besides, virtually everyone active online would ping as a freak and not deliver in person.

Speaking of not delivering, Grocery Cart is now sitting in the meditation room, pressing her palms against the carpet. I don't know yoga from toga, but I'm pretty sure that isn't what she's doing. Maybe it's just bumping into her at a store that makes her action look like she's testing the carpet for installation in her home. I don't know what her deal is, but I can see the reduced fee ahead.

Otherwise, everything looks normal, so I turn from the mirror and tell the voice I'm ready to go.

"Please standby," says the voice. Not Majel, but the *Lost in Space* robot. Although it is less unsettling than HAL 9000 would be, the combined change in voice and request is ominous. This has not happened before. I don't try the door, afraid it might be locked, but even more afraid of verifying that it is.

"Sure. No problem," I say in a failed attempt to sound casual. With nowhere else to focus my attention while I standby, I look back through the mirror. Grocery Cart is nowhere to be seen. As I wait for the refund request, I notice the door to one of the personal quarters is closed.

"Thank you for waiting."

"Sure. Can I speak with Majel, please?"

"Majel is occupied."

"Hey," I say. "If this is about the one female captive who isn't working out, I'm sorry. I'm not sure how she got into the mix. She barely registered. But I take full responsibility and will give a full refund."

"Something has come to our attention." The voice ignores my suggestion. "We have other harvesting options."

Other harvesting options? I wonder. *What's that mean?*

"We would like to renegotiate."

"Um, sure," I say. "I was thinking it was about time to do that just moments ago." Not a lie, but the crab rangoons are out for sure. "What were you thinking?"

"Offer a reduced fee. Other concessions are advised."

Other concessions? I think. *What? Give up my "LAVATORY?"*

I stare at the closed door beyond the mirror. "What are you up to?" I wonder aloud, thinking back through her actions. The carpet. The food. Then it dawns on me. My mind replays what I thought was her self-examination in the mirror. She tugged at her eye with her middle finger. She wasn't checking the bags there, she was flipping me off.

"We are waiting," says the voice.

"Who is she?" I ask, knowing the voice won't answer. "And why does she get to talk to Majel?"

"Your offer, please."

"Seventy-five percent of my current rate," I say, then add, "and you can remove the LAVATORY." *I'll pee in the corner if I have to.*

"One moment."

And the voice is quiet for exactly one moment—just long enough for me to replay the grocery cart collision. She didn't run into me as I had originally remembered. I headed down the wrong aisle, diapers on one side, grampers on the other. Despite what you're thinking, I didn't need or want to be there. So I spun my cart around to retreat and crashed my cart headlong into hers. She apologized, but it was "totally my fault," I said, and apologized up and down. *Not! I now realize.*

"Is that your final offer?" asks the voice. It doesn't say the offer isn't good enough, but the question itself tells me all I need to know.

"Sixty percent and no LAVATORY, but I get fresh crab rangoons here in the viewing room and can borrow games from the captives' library." I'm negotiating the wrong direction, but am fed up. Besides, board games are expensive. Then, I add the poison pill. "And you must fully disclose who you are and the nature of this operation."

"Is that your final offer?"

Not even a request for a moment to consider or counter. "I'm not removing the audit clause, if that's what you're after."

"Is that your final offer?"

"Yes. Final offer. And non-negotiable."

"Thank you. We will be in touch," the voice says as the door to the viewing room opens with a loud click and buzzing sound, like a jail cell. Don't ask how I know. My criminal law class visited one.

I walk to the teleporter, knowing it is the last time. There is no door marked "LAVATORY" along the corridor, confirming what I already know. "Don't hesitate to contact me if you need anything, Majel," I say as I step onto the glowing circle.

Apparently, the contract was awarded to the lowest bidder—maybe that isn't just a U.S. government practice. Or is it? I still don't know.

At least I got paid my full fee for Grocery Cart—I'm avoiding the other names I have for her. It was time I would have to seek a new orbit to attract freaks, and I didn't want to move, anyway.

When I get home, I open my phone to delete the MB contact. It's there, between "George" and "Mom." "Auto Shop" and "Doctor" are the only entries above that. I change my mind. If... when they come crawling back for my help, it will certainly be the Majel voice. And I would start the negotiations at my full fee and the conditions where I left them, poison pill and all.

Instead, I touch the entry for George, a local friend.

"Hey George," I say when he answers. "You want to watch my *Twilight Zone* collection tonight?"

About Eccentric Orbit

Eccentric Orbit is the second story, the right bookend, in the *Abduction Coordinator* bookend series. If you haven't already, be sure to read the companion story, *Freak Magnet*, to get the full picture. Sometimes the concept for a story is as simple as a word or phrase that sounds like it should be a story title, which was the case with *Eccentric Orbit*.

Prompt

I just liked the term and imagined a story about space beings with eccentric cargo.

Inspiration

The meat of the story developed was a natural extension to the story *Freak Magnet* and the nerd fanaticism over the popular culture icons mentioned. Though critical of the "freaks," the protagonist is exposed as a bit of a freak, too.

The story doesn't reveal the nature of the captors, so you can decide for yourself. Due to an extensive non-disclosure agreement, I won't say who they really are.

Easter Egg

I am a boardgame designer and game afficionado who loves to "unbox" and "punch" the components (pop them out of their temporary frames) of new games. And yes, I am a card "sleever," which is bonus nerd cred.

Full Disclosure: For Sale: Haunted House

PG: Ghosts, Humorous, Mainstream

Frank watched through the picture window as two cars parked at the curb out front, Marge's gold Caddie, she called it champagne, and a white Lexus SUV.

"Time for me to move on. Okay?" This was the fourth time Frank said this into the empty room, and the umpteenth time he had shown the house.

Selling the old place had become a part-time job. Marge had offered to show it while Frank was at work, but no telling what would happen without him there.

Marge escorted a middle-aged couple to the front door, waving her arms as she pointed out features of the yard and neighborhood. She made a big arching point toward the west.

They don't care about the school, Marge. They better not.

It was Marge's habit to include the school in her litany of gestures, but Frank had told her "no kids." She argued it was a great kids' yard, and the school right there—at the end of her swooping point.

"Limiting your options," she had said.

"No kids." Frank was adamant. Unloading the place on unsuspecting adults was bad enough. He couldn't live with himself if kids moved in. He invented a story about it being the wrong neighborhood, which was belied by the tree fort out back. "It isn't safe," he had told her. He should tear it down, but that wouldn't happen. Frank's back twinged, waiting there behind the front door, reminding him of the fall he took when he had tried.

Since the second showing, Frank waited for Marge to ring the bell, then a few seconds more, before opening the door. He had opened the door on that second couple as their gazes followed Marge's swooping point and startled them. Despite his apologies, they looked over their shoulders the entire walkthrough. The strange smells didn't help.

Frank opened the door—not too fast, not creepy-slow. *Please don't creak.*

For all their greetings here at the door, Marge's over-the-top "hello" became less genuine each time. Maybe fewer minutes on the makeup and a few more on the hair would help. Her hair was such a fright.

Marge made introductions as Frank invited them in, but Frank forgot their names before he even closed the door. *Tim or Tom and Autumn. Or was it Spring?* One of many reasons Frank needed Marge.

While the couple asked questions, Frank sneaked in his own.

"Do you have any pets? A cat maybe?" Though Frank had told Marge "no cats," he needed to hear it. At least, have it confirmed in the house.

"Allergic to cats," said Tim-Tom. He turned his head to the side and took a wrinkled-nose sniff. "You haven't had cats in here, have you?"

Spring made a face that said the cat ban wouldn't last, but hopefully the man's response was enough.

Frank wasn't the only one who needed to hear their responses.

"No. No cats," said Frank, leading them down the hall. "Or dogs." *Not for years, anyway. Is there a statute of limitations for animal occupancy?* The cat lived in perpetual fear, so moved to the neighbor's. Missy, Frank's dog, was routinely tempted into mischief and got blamed for everything. So Frank's sister took her in until he found a new place.

Frank tripped over... nothing, hitting his head on a door frame. He was still paying for taking the dog away.

"Good," said the man. Then, looking at Autumn, "Maybe a small dog someday. A cavapoo or something hypoallergenic. One that won't destroy the lawn."

Good answer. A cavapoo would be perfect.

"Do the appliances stay?" asked Tim-Tom, stroking the fridge door.

"Fingerprints, Tom," scolded Autumn.

Better get used to those.

Tom buffed the door with his shirtsleeve. "They stay?"

Yes, please, thought Frank. But Marge had warned free means junk. "They're negotiable."

"They all work?"

"Yes." *Even when you don't turn them on.*

"The garbage disposal, too?" asked Tom, his hand poised over the kitchen sink.

"No! I mean, yes. Give it a go. Just don't put your hand..."

Tom flipped the switch and lowered his hand toward the grinding drain until everyone's knees buckled to his satisfaction.

As the tour moved to the utility room, Tom rubbed his hands together, then laid them on the sides of the water heater like he was using an AED. "Of course, we'll have this all inspected, but have you had any problems with the water heater?"

"Works great." *You might take a freezing shower when it gets turned off mysteriously in the middle of the night.*

"The furnace?" *The furnace got a Vulcan mind-meld.*

"Heats this place right up," said Frank. *Especially in the hottest days of summer. Summer! That's her name.* "AC, too. It's turned off for the season, though." *And I couldn't afford the electricity to turn the house into a fridge.*

The tour went better than most. *No unexplained noises, flickering lights.* Frank was ready for the sale. "Are you familiar with the area?" *Please no.*

"No," said Summer. "My job just moved here. Tom can work anywhere."

Let's hope so. "So, you work from home, Tom? I figured you for an engineer."

"That obvious?" He laughed, patting his shirt pocket. "I took out the pocket protector."

Yeah, that obvious. "Just how you knew so much about the furnace."

"Two degrees. Engineering and law. I'm a product safety and liability consultant."

"Sounds interesting." *Shit!*

"Actually, I noticed the treehouse. Class action on that brand. Can't believe you haven't taken it down. Attractive nuisance, they call that."

"I would have, but I'm not mechanically inclined." Frank's trip in the hall made this an easy sell. Despite the cost, he was glad his vast assortment of tools were in storage, where he didn't need to explain them. Marge said an empty garage showed better.

"If you saw the sadistics, you'd tear it down. One step below a trauma-leen." Tom laughed at Frank's obvious bewilderment. "Tramp-o-line."

"Ah, yes." Frank laughed along, being courteous.

"Seems I read something about a horrible treehouse accident in this neighborhood."

"Really?"

"Did the lights just flicker?"

About Full Disclosure

Many haunted house stories are about people insisting on staying in a house despite the constant fear of and harassment from the ghosts. *Full Disclosure* flips that trope on its head. The ghost apparently won't let Frank leave unless it approves of the new residents. Frank knows the ghost's criteria and tries to support some and thwart others (like bringing a dog into the house for the ghost to play with rather than a cat to terrorize).

Prompt

What troubles would you have while selling a haunted house? Especially if the ghost likes you and doesn't want you to leave.

Inspiration

One of my favorite moments in the story is the scene with the garbage disposal. I'm one of *those* people (and I know I'm not alone) who are freaky about putting their hand in the dish drain. My parents must have ground that danger-fear into me and it has stuck to this day.

Derelict in Space: Suspicious Survey

PG: Aliens, Ghosts, Humorous, Sci-Fi

Right Bookend: Age of Sail in Space

Oort Cloud, 5 February, Earth Year 2380

"Captain, we're picking up an object on the long-range. Could be a ship."

The captain could see and do everything she needed from her command couch, but a potential ship was something to be shared. She stood up and walked to look over Navigation Officer Chun's shoulder at his console. "Drive signature?"

"None we can detect. It's not burning at present, ma'am."

"Why do you think it's a ship?" She leaned closer.

"Its course. Straight out of the system."

"Looks like its speed is constant. Could it be ejecta?"

"Possible, but I don't think so. It would be uncanny for this lone piece to have such a direct course out of the system." Chun's fingers tapped busily on the console interface.

"A probe, then?"

"That's what it looks like. Or a derelict. I'm running the sim now based on current course and speed." He pointed at his second screen, which was flashing several series of numbers representing time and location. "May take a while."

Of course, Chun was already running the sim. He always anticipated the next question. "You think it's from Earth?" asked the captain.

"That's my bet."

"What's its size?"

"About forty meters. We'd need to get closer, to be more exact."

"Forty meters? How'd you find that on the long-range?"

"It just happened to cross our survey window and fit the harvest profile."

"Right, just happened. Let's get a closer look, but go easy. I don't believe in coincidences."

Not to be left out of the conversation, the first mate piped in, "Searching records all the way back to the first documented launch. There are a couple from the nineteen seventies out here, but no documented probes should be in this sector now."

"Plenty of undocumented launches out there," said the captain. "Chun, your bet is still Earth origin?"

"I'll give two-to-one it is."

The captain chuckled. "Not likely to find any takers, Chun."

"I'll take that," said the first mate. "Nothing else exciting up here."

Science Officer Pok finally had something to contribute to the conversation. "Within range. Scanning for life forms." Everyone was quiet, waiting for the results. "No life forms, but picking up evidence of Zert tech."

"Zerts. Shoulda known," said the captain. "Tricky bastards. Be careful on approach."

"I hate those insectoids," said Chun with unusual vehemence. Probably because his bet wasn't looking good. "The way they chirp by rubbing their legs. Yuh. I can't hear a cricket without cringing."

"Fortunately, there aren't many crickets on a mining survey ship," said Pok flatly.

"I'll see if the replicator has the recipe," sniped Chun.

"Focus," said the captain. "We may have a situation at hand." The warning wasn't necessary, but like the banter between the officers, her reminders were expected decorum.

"We have a visual," said Pok. "Putting on the main screen now."

"What the..." they said in unison.

"Obviously not Zert tech," said the captain.

"Its shields are definitely Zert. Could be a cloak," said Chun. "Has to be."

"If we can believe our eyes, we don't need the results of your calculation," said the first mate. "It obviously has an Earth origin."

Just then, Chun's second screen flashed its result, accompanied by a "bing." "Origin: Earth. Launch Date: 5 February 1880. Accuracy: 98.76%."

"Nine eight seven six, huh? What's the date today?" the captain asked everyone on the bridge.

Pok started to reply first. "Star date—"

"I mean Earth date," she interrupted.

Though the Gregorian calendar was meaningless anywhere but Earth, humans throughout the solar system still used it. It's just in space, without the handy floor mats they use on passenger ships, it's easy to lose track.

"It isn't April first, if that's what you're thinking," said Chun. He looked at his watch. "Fifth of February, twenty-three, eighty." Then he looked at his screen again. "Exactly five hundred years."

"Captain, there's movement aboard that ship," said Pok.

"I thought you said no lifeforms."

"Still not detecting any."

"Droids, then?"

Pok zoomed the image on the main screen to show translucent figures moving around on the surface of the ship. "Not sure what you'd call them. They appear to be cloaked. Transparent to most of the visible spectrum."

"What does her hull say?" asked the captain, but if the rest of this scenario played out as expected, real or contrived, she already knew.

Pok panned the main screen image to the fore of the ship's hull and zoomed in on its identification. "HMS *Atalanta.*"

The captain stared at the screen in silence.

"Captain Stirling?" prompted Chun.

Pok continued, "Wikipedia shows the HMS *Atalanta* disappeared somewhere off a Caribbean island called Bermuda in Gregorian year 1880. Destination was Falmouth in the country then called England. The ship was assumed a wreck and sunk in the Atlantic."

"Yes, I know," said the captain.

"The captain was..." Pok looked at the captain. "Stirling..."

"That's the ship you have framed on your cabin wall," said the first mate.

"Match course and prepare to board," said Stirling, moving toward the lift.

"Do we dare?" Asked Chun. "If it's not a Zert trap, it's literally a ghost ship. Maybe both."

"That's my ancestor aboard that ship," she said. "I'm boarding her. I need one other."

The first mate jumped into line behind the captain. "I'm game," he said. "Finally, some excitement."

"Suit up then, Adamson. I want to speak to her captain if I can. Maybe I can clear his name."

About Derelict in Space

Derelict in Space is the second story, the right bookend, of the *Age of Sail in Space* bookend stories. An interesting fact of the series is the concept for the second story came first. In case you skipped it, be sure to read the left bookend story, *Souls at Sea*, to get the full picture.

Prompt

What if intergalactic explorers came across a ghost ship? One from the Age of Sail.

Inspiration

As I developed the story, I considered the events that resulted in the ship traveling through space, which led to the bookend story, *Souls at Sea: A Bermuda Training Voyage.*

As a fan of both speculative and historical fiction, the prospect of the mash-up set an intriguing course for my imaginative journey. While it may seem improbable that the descendants of the *Atalanta* crew discovered the ghost ship—everything else about the story is completely believable—I thought it a reasonable rationale for why the ship was discovered when it was.

Alien Factory: Rite of Ascension

PG: Aliens, Sci-Fi, Serious, YA

Bik sat on the riverbank, wiping his forehead, and looking through sweat-teared eyes across the river at the alien factory.

"Hey, Bik." Lurt called from across the furgeball field behind him.

"Yeah," Bik said to the open air ahead of him, but Lurt couldn't hear him over the roar of the river.

"Bik? Did you find the ball?"

"Yeah," he called over his shoulder, "it's right here." Bik pointed toward the river below.

"Well? Can you get it?"

"In a minute."

Pretending disgust, Lurt asked, "You tired already?" But he didn't mind the rest. The two boys usually played hard for half the day before taking a break, but he got winded easily today. He walked across the faintly lined field toward Bik and the ball and the factory across the river.

Bik turned his attention back to the factory until he heard Lurt's footsteps coming close. "Just taking a breather."

"Good idea," said Lurt. "Where's the ball?"

"Down there." Bik pointed at the hand-sized leather saucer near the water.

"You don't suppose it's getting wet, do you?"

"No. Stop worrying about the furgeball and sit down."

"No sweat." Lurt sat down. "What's bugging you? Your mom still sick?"

"Yeah, it's bad. Your little sister?"

"Fussing and crying. She wouldn't even nurse this morning."

"They'll get better," said Bik. The boys sat quietly for a few moments before he said, "Something about that factory bothers me."

"Of course it bothers you. It bothers me. We have no idea what goes on over there. What's new about that?"

"Something else. I know what goes on over there."

"You do, huh? Then please explain it to the rest of us. No one else in the village seems to know."

"The elders know. My father knows. But they're afraid to say anything, or even think about it, because everyone else will call them crazy."

"*You're* crazy."

"See."

"So, what *are* they doing over there?" Lurt was serious.

"I'm not *completely* sure anymore."

"Aw, you had me going."

"Listen. That's what bugs me. The aliens came here to take something they needed from the ground, and they've been shipping it home at night. But something's changed."

"Like what?"

"Look at how many aliens are over there now."

"Yeah, there's more every day. So?"

"And the number of flying ships every night has gone up."

"Have they? I don't even hear them anymore."

"How can you sleep..." Bik turned toward Lurt. "The ships bring more aliens and carry away the treasure."

"How do you know what they do at night? The fires aren't bright enough to see over there."

"You just agreed there are more of them... They come from somewhere... Where do you think the aliens come from?" Bik asked as if the question had just popped into his head, but he'd been wondering a long time.

"I try not to think about it. We're not supposed to."

"Those things over there are aliens."

"Of course they're aliens. They work at the *alien* factory."

"I mean real aliens. From-another-world aliens."

"See, you *are* crazy." Lurt stood and started easing his way down the bank to retrieve his ball.

"My dad said when they first came here, they had to wear protective suits. Explain that."

"They were afraid of catching something from us. Like a disease they didn't have in their village," he said. Then, looking straight at Bik, "Like crazy fever. We've had visitors from other villages who've had the same fear."

"Maybe, but why did they take the suits off?"

"They figured out..." Lurt grunted as he reached for the ball. "They weren't going to catch anything."

"And how did they find that out? You ever hear of one coming over here and asking?"

"No. I don't know. They're just smarter than we are."

"Exactly. A lot smarter." Bik stood to give Lurt a hand up the steep bank. "We should build a boat and go over there. See what they're doing on our world."

"You know that's forbidden. Besides, by the time you paddled across, you'd be a half-day's walk downstream. Then you'd have to walk all the way over there." Lurt gestured toward the factory. "Back to your boat, cross the river, and walk a day to get back here. You'd be gone... four days or more. That's if the *aliens* didn't eat you."

Bik looked at the river current, the distance to the factory, and worked out the days in his head. "Yeah, you're right. I still want a better look at them." He thought of a way to do it, but didn't say anything.

"I'm nervous enough watching them from here."

"You're nervous *now*? Take a good look over there today. Look again tomorrow or the next day. See if there isn't a change."

Lurt looked at the immense factory with the vehicles and figures moving around it. "There are a lot of them over there these days, but it isn't the first time they've been busy."

"You're right," said Bik. "But it's the first time it hasn't slowed back down." He grabbed the ball from Lurt. "They're getting ready for something... something big." Turning away from the river and the mystery of the factory, he jogged toward the center of the field.

Lurt looked again at the busy factory. "He's just trying to scare me," he thought aloud before running after Bik. "Hey, wait up."

The next offday the two friends met, as always, at the old furgeball field. They played here, despite the rocks and divots, instead of at the newer field away from the river where the other kids played. The new field was safer except the kids there were more interested in the violence than the strategy of the once ritualistic sport.

When asked why they played at the old field, Bik always answered with the half-truth, "Gotta keep an eye on those aliens." Lurt was nervous about playing by the river, by the factory, but was only interested in playing a good game instead of brawling with the others. That is, until this offday.

As they approached the center of the field to begin the game, Lurt eyed the factory carefully. He saw no aliens.

"Weird, huh?" said Bik.

"Yeah. What do you think is up?"

"Got me, but it can't be good."

"You don't suppose they all left?" Lurt walked toward the river, forgetting about the game.

"According to my dad," said Bik. "They appeared overnight and built that huge factory in a matter of days. I imagine they could leave overnight."

"Maybe they got what they wanted and left."

"One problem."

"No ships last night." Lurt smiled at his deduction, but it soon faded.

"Not a noise in the sky. They're still over there, but something's gone wrong... What's that?" Bik pointed at a bright reflective object creeping around the corner of the largest building. He took his father's seefar tube from his pocket and watched the aliens through it. A parade of silvery figures moved around the main building and through the entrance of another, smaller building.

"Hey, your father will kill you if he sees you with that," said Lurt. But he snatched the tube out of Bik's hand when he offered it. "Must be some kind of vehicle," he said, looking through the tube. "There's another... and another."

"Those are the aliens in their suits."

"Can't be. They're..."

"My father said they didn't look like they could even be human in those suits."

Lurt nodded in agreement and handed the seefar tube back to Bik. "Some of them have four arms."

"They tricked us when they weren't in the suits," said Bik. He watched the last of the alien procession disappear into the building before putting the tube back in his pocket. "I hope they're not wearing those suits for the reason I'm thinking."

"Yeah. How are you feeling, Bik?"

"Kinda queasy." Bik tried to swallow the taste of bile from his mouth. "You?"

"Same." Lurt held the ball in the air between them. "Let's play."

"For rites, this time." Bik stood on one side of the central circle and held his hands high overhead. Lurt stood, opposing him, and dropped the ball into a smaller circle between them.

"For rites," said Lurt. "Like our fathers did." He locked his fingers with Bik's, then kicked the ball.

The boys played the ritual game until the sun was setting and the sky above screamed with flying ships. Bik and Lurt watched from the field, the ball between them, as ships landed at the factory, loaded silver aliens, then quickly returned to flight. As the last ship raced toward the stars, the sky over the factory flared to daylight.

The boys never heard the explosion.

About Alien Factory

Alien Factory is the most serious of the stories in the series—in the grand tradition of using a sci-fi setting to consider a disturbing contemporary issue. Though the original issue considered took place in 1984, the story is as relevant today as ever.

Prompt

What would it be like living next to a technology you don't understand when it goes horribly awry?

Inspiration

Unfortunately, the prompt came from actual events, the catastrophic "Bhopal disaster" or "Bhopal gas tragedy" in December 1984. An accident at the Union Carbide India Limited (UCIL) pesticide plant in Bhopal, Madhya Pradesh, India released toxic gases which killed over 3,700 and injured over 570,000 unsuspecting residents in the region. The incident is still considered the world's worst industrial disaster, immediately affecting almost 100 times as many people as the Chernobyl disaster.

The news covered the incident extensively, but I was also a chemistry major at the time (later to become an environmental laboratory scientist and manager), so I was influenced and distraught by the tragedy. I drafted the story shortly after the event and developed it over a year or two. I revised the current version for this collection in 2022.

Most of the changes reflect how I have matured as a writer. I tried to keep the final version as close as possible to the raw original. One interesting change I made was to the name of the game the boys play. I originally called the game "quidge" and the ball was a "quidge ball." Little did I know in 1985 that this silly name could be confused as stolen from a popular fantasy story. The actual name was unimportant, so I changed it to "furgeball."

The "Rite of Ascension" subtitle brings attention to a dichotomy in the story. As boys, Bik and Lurt, understand and practice a rite of maturity. But as a species, the aliens had ascended beyond their maturity. The boys ascend to adulthood as the alien ships ascend to space.

Easter Egg

The "seefar" is an item in my Alpineland setting for the *Hero Kids Fantasy RPG* with artwork by Brian Phongluangtham. Bik and Lurt are "hero kids."

Mending Time: A Line to the Past

PG: Ghosts, Historical, Holiday, Mainstream, Mystery, Portal

Part 1: The Window

Robert had lived in the apartment nearly two weeks before he noticed the clothesline out his window—the simple cord from which hung his future. Even then, he didn't discover it by looking out the window. The blinds were down when he moved in, and when he tried to raise them that first morning, they started to buckle. So, he left them alone, now hanging at a slant from pulling on them, and hoped they didn't fall off the wall.

The window faced a narrow alley anyway, and the view was the wall of an old factory, blackened from a fire a hundred years ago. Though it would be indirect, more sunlight in the dark studio would be nice. But the blinds down would have to do, yellowed as they were with age and smoke-stain from previous occupants—they obviously couldn't blow their smoke out the window of the supposed non-smoking apartment.

After a walk around the neighborhood, looking for a public phone, Robert ambled up the alley. He had a cell phone, but with his pay-as-you-go plan and diminishing ability to do the pay part, he reserved it for taking calls and texts. Hopefully, one from the library to schedule a job interview. He dropped off his application three days ago already. Though, they helpfully suggested a response would be faster if he applied online, which he could do from one of the computers available there at the library.

Taking the alley wasn't part of Robert's walk-about-the neighborhood plan. It was just the shortest, and smelliest, route back to the front of his building. As he walked through the alley, he looked up, which was unusual these days. He was always looking at his feet, especially while dodging the garbage and oil-slicked puddles of the alley. Maybe a plane flew over. He didn't remember.

But he looked up. And saw the shirts and skirts and trousers and towels of his neighbors overhead, hanging to dry on lines strung between the buildings. Most of the lines hung slack, and some were missing—even in this low-rent building, most tenants probably used the coin-op laundromat three blocks down. Not their bathtub.

Each apartment had only one window, so finding his was a simple matter of counting windows above as he did doors in his hallway. Three up and three from the end. Though the light in the alley was dim and the angle steep, Robert thought he could see the blinds askew through the grimy glass. He felt a little embarrassed. But assessing his outward appearance to the world wasn't his purpose. At the moment.

Mounted on the wall, next to his window, was a pulley. Through it was strung a cord, suspended from a similar pulley on the other building. Other than the four pigeons resting there in the shade of the alley, there was nothing hanging out on the line. Though it was cool in the shaded alley compared to most of the city, the breeze created by the narrow gap would air-dry clothes much faster than hanging them over the shower rod. And not clutter his bathroom.

When Robert opened his apartment door, he went straight to the window, eased the bottom of the blinds away from the glass, and peeked through the triangle of daylight. The view was fuzzy behind the film on the glass, but the clothesline was there, proving he could count to three, and at least two of the pigeons. The line extended beyond the edge of his triangle, but was no doubt still attached to the factory wall, and likely still supported another pigeon or two.

Robert glared over his shoulder at the coat and pants hanging from the shower rod and the shirts bent over the back of his two folding, dining chairs, drying with a mid-riff crease. Then he went to work with a screwdriver he borrowed from the landlord. He removed the blinds.

Robert laid them on the folding card table that had been his grandmother's, where she had played endless hands of canasta, where he daily searched the want ads in always yesterday's paper, and where he now cleaned and repaired the blinds, plucking the age-old dust bunnies from the track, untangling the cords, and scrubbing away the grime with his holiest of socks and soapy water.

When satisfied, Robert took the paired sock and re-matched it with the other, scrubbing the grime off the sash window, revealing the span of line that stretched to the old factory. Through his clean window he could see the far pulley was anchored in the old factory near a window, dark in the daylight, with a dark drape hanging behind it. The shock of yellow brick, where setting the anchor had shattered the fire-blackened wall, shone like a starburst in the night.

When Robert tried to open the window, his hands flew up, and he banged the back of one on the upper frame. But the window didn't budge. By the globs of old paint, laced with smooth channels like eroded canyons, the gap between the window and the frame had been painted over and cracked and painted over again several times since the window had been opened last. And never scraped.

Robert was thankful he had endured the landlord's questioning about his intended use of the screwdriver before handing it over, holding it there between them like a biscuit before a dog that must sit up. He used the point of it to cut and scrape and chisel the paint from the gap, using the palm of his hand as a hammer. He had mentioned none of these uses to the landlord.

Robert peeled the layers back—one an ugly peach-pink, but most various shades of off-white, eggshell and antique, as surely all were now—exposing the dark oak beneath. When he finished, he admired his reflection in the window framed with a thin line of red-brown raw wood. Then he pried the sash free.

The window opened. Not easily, but it opened. And closed. The counterweights were long gone, their cords surely rotted away, but the window was sticky in the frame, requiring effort to raise or lower it. With a few tests, Robert convinced himself the heavy sash wouldn't guillotine him while leaning out into the open air of the alley.

In what became Robert's final test, he was feeding the line through the pulley, inspecting the cord for frays and critter nibbles, picking off the pigeon poop and a few old wooden pins even, wondering if he could use vegetable oil on the squeaking pulley, when his phone rang. The phone was sitting on the once card table, now workbench, and it was ringing. Robert jerked back and banged his head on the glass before slipping through the window, which stayed open. But there was no time to celebrate.

One hand massaging the back of his head, Robert picked up the phone with the other, flipping it open with his thumb. It rang again in his palm. Wasn't it supposed to answer when he opened it? He tried to remember which button to push to answer while fighting the urge to open the settings.

"Hello," he said, raising the phone to his ear, hoping the ringing had stopped because he pushed the right button, not that the caller had given up. *Don't give up.* A voice.

"Yes, it is... Tomorrow morning is fine... My calendar just opened up as well... Yes, I know where it is... Yes, that was me... No, I'm good with computers. Used them in my research... I'm new to the area and wanted to see the library anyway... Excellent. Tomorrow at ten, then... Goodbye."

As soon as Robert hung up, he tested the dampness of his interview clothes, where they hung hopefully from the shower rod. They weren't drying fast enough in the muggy apartment, so the timing of finding the clothesline couldn't have been better. He shuttled the clothes from the bathroom and chair backs to the window, pinning them on the line with the old pins he trusted not to break and from hangers fastened to the line with bits of string. He needed clothespins.

With each new garment pinned, Robert watched the parade of clothes bob in the void between buildings as he fed out the line. When all his clothes hung from the line now sagging in a shallow arc, he realized he was trusting the line not to break and the pigeons not to return to do what pigeons do.

He also noticed that a person could reach the clothesline through the awning window on the other side. Surely, he needn't worry about someone stealing his laundry. In these times, you never knew, but no one would want to steal his worn shirts and threadbare pants and coat. He eyed the window, anyway, watching for the slightest movement of the drab, black drape hanging behind it.

When satisfied there was no one at the other end, he rehung the blinds, returned the screwdriver, resisting the desire to tease the landlord with it. Back in the apartment, he boiled water for tea and ramen, which he ate at the card table while torturing his mind with potential interview questions and trying to remember the rules for canasta.

In the morning, Robert hadn't thought about the extra time it would take to retrieve his clothes from the line, and he had already dawdled about, which he only did when something important loomed ahead. He polished his shoes, which he had polished the night before, scraped a bit of gum off the sole of one, no doubt from the alley, fiddled with a snaggy fingernail, and worried his thumb over the bruise in his palm-hammer, testing how little pressure was enough to make it hurt.

So, Robert was in such a rush and such a worried state over being late to the interview, he threw the clothes on without looking at them. In the hurried glance, the shirt and pants looked unrumpled enough that he needn't iron them and be any later. He supposed the breeze in the alley, warm from the accumulated sun bake on all the concrete of the city, must have acted like a steam press. Anyway, there was no time to think about it now. He had to get to that interview.

It wasn't until Robert returned home and was hanging the coat in the closet that he noticed the seam in the shoulder, the one that had been pulling apart, wasn't showing the exposed threads of his attempted repair, like the laces on a shoe. The seam was as neat and tidy as it had been when he bought the coat a dozen plus years, four apartments, and three jobs ago, if you didn't count the day work. The other shoulder, which was also pulling apart, but not so much he thought it needed repair yet, was just as neat and tight as the other.

These changes were subtle enough that he excused overlooking them in his rush to get to the interview. But the new contrasting patches over the worn elbows... The baffling comment from the interviewer and research department head, Ms. Bernard, who asked to be called Jane, now made some little sense. "I like your style, Robert," she said as she ushered him to the library entrance.

On closer inspection, the shirts and pants, also, had not just dried flat. They had been mended and starched and pressed, and in the corner of each crisp shirt tail was stitched a simple monogram, "MTZ." Obviously, not Robert's initials, which was a relief. That would be creepy if whoever mended his shirts knew his name.

Part 2: The Museum

Robert dashed the four steps to the window and raised the blinds with a jerk. He didn't think about it until later, but fortunately, they didn't crash down on his head. His repairs were sound.

The clothesline looked as it had before. Two of the pigeons had returned—the rust and white one and the dappled gray. And the window across the alley next to where the line rounded the pulley anchored in the starburst chipped, soot-black wall? Now that Robert looked more carefully, the wall wasn't just black. Waves of black and charcoal gray mimicked the flames that had painted it there, framing the window.

The window. It was still closed, and the drab black drape still hung behind it, like the drab black drapes hanging behind all the windows on the second and third floors—the ground floor an uninterrupted wall of blackened brick. Nothing had changed.

Robert leaned out the window and looked at the clotheslines up and down the alley, lacing the buildings together. He judged the distance to the pocked pavement below. Only Philippe Petit could get to Robert's clothesline, and he probably didn't sew. It wasn't the famous "Man on Wire" mending Robert's clothes, but someone in the old factory. Through the window.

The *new* window. The old building had been reglazed at some point. In Robert's tours of the neighborhood, he hadn't walked past the entrance on the opposite side of the building. What was it now? Apartments? Apartments with heavy black drapes in all the windows? Like tonight's laundry plan, tomorrow's walk-about plan was set.

After another meal of tea and ramen, Robert kneeled before the tub and washed the shirt and pants he had worn the day before while fixing the window and blinds. Both were covered with the dust and grime of the blinds and window and were spotted with dry paint flecks. The shirt smelled of the sweat it took to pry the window loose.

Robert would have given up on these as rags, had he replacements, so washed two more shirts that still had some life for his test. As the night before, he hung them on the line, and as before, the pulley squeaked with each pull on the return line.

As the sun set, Robert lowered the blind most of the way. Then, he scooched his one armchair to the window and positioned himself in it so he could look through the slice of exposed window. Waiting for something to happen, he traced the upholstery pattern on the chair's arm until his snaggy fingernail caught a loose thread and widened a hole where myriad elbows had worn the material thin and through. Too bad he couldn't hang the armchair on the line. But it wouldn't fit through the window.

When it grew dark outside and inside the apartment, Robert clipped a small reading light to the window ledge and started reading one of two books he had checked out after the interview. The guide on interview skills from 650.14 sat ignored on the card table—the objective was to stay awake—while he read the book from 974.71, a history of the fire that destroyed the factory at the end of his clothes-line and claimed the lives of its employees. Mostly women. Mostly seamstresses.

Apparently, not even the historical tragedy kept Robert awake because when he opened his eyes, the book was closed in his lap and the pulley outside his window was creaking. Glad he hadn't tried the vegetable oil, he clicked off the lamp. The pulley stopped creaking. Just as he was certain he had foiled his own trap, the pulley started squeaking again. He leaned toward the window until his nose touched the sill.

A dim, blue-green light illuminated the factory window. A replica moon reflected off the angled pane of the open awning window. The blue-white moonlight illuminated Robert's one remaining shirt on the line. The white, now blue like the moon, shirt bobbed and drift-ed toward the far window like a happy trick-or-treater. As the shirt reached the far pulley, the creaking stopped, and the shirt vanished through the triangle gap of the awning window.

Mere moments later, the shirt reappeared, and now Robert could see the hands clipping it to the line and the arms reaching through the window and the figure of a person, appearing translucent in the reflected moonlight, a woman in an apron with her hair tied back. The pulley creaked as the shirt drifted toward him. Then, one by one, the colored linen shirts and pleated pants reappeared on the line. With the final creak of the pulley, the awning closed with a "thunk." The light faded from the window.

Despite the anxiety, and maybe in part because of it, waiting until daylight won Robert's internal debate on when to retrieve the clothes. Staring out the window, book in his lap, he fell asleep in the chair.

Robert awoke to daylight leaking through the gap beneath the blinds and his phone ringing, this time in his pocket. He fished it out, knocking the book to the floor, flipped the phone open, and said, "Hello," confident he had found the correct setting to "answer on open."

"Good morning," came the now familiar voice of Ms. Bernard.

"Good morning... Yes, I can... Perfect... I look forward to our conversation... Thank you... Goodbye."

Robert closed the phone and fretted over the open question. He hadn't thought about an appropriate salary. What he referred to as reserve, and denied as fear of failure, had prevented him from thinking along that path. And suddenly, he needed to be well down that path. And though he was going to the library, he didn't have time to find a resource to guide him on that path. He'd have to wing it because first, he must visit the old factory.

Resting his elbows on his knees, Robert peered out the window, down the string of his clothes hanging like semaphores from the line. His gaze dropped to the book on the floor, which had fallen open to a page with a photo of the factory employees, mostly women wearing dark dresses and white aprons, their hair pulled back and tied up with ribbons to keep it out of the machinery. Dresses and aprons and hair pulled back, like the woman in the window.

Robert inspected the garments as he brought them in off the line. Each was clean and pressed and mended as before. Each embroidered with the monogram "MTZ." With reverence befitting vestments, he hung them neatly in the closet.

Without having to reposition clothes from the rod, Robert showered, then "dressed for success"—he had noticed some such title while scanning the shelves for the interview guide.

The sun greeted Robert as he left the building, then warmed his back as he turned down the block toward the factory. He walked briskly, matching pace with the crowd on the sidewalk, but stepped to the side to stop at the alley entrance.

Even to him, who knew the alley possessed something peculiar, the view was uninteresting. He merged back into the flow and walked around to the front of the factory, where he entered a tunnel of scaffold and chain link and graffitied plywood, tagged and retagged at odd angles with symbols meaningless to him.

A gap opened in the chain link and spray-painted plywood at the factory entrance, and though Robert was looking for it, the crowd nearly pushed him past it before he could spill into the alcove of scaffold. Neatly lettered in gold on the entrance door glass was "Shirtwaist Factory Museum and Lofts." Another sign on white posterboard hung in the window. "Coming Soon. Premium Lofts. Starting in the low..." followed by a figure Robert could never afford. But he could follow the instructions to "inquire inside."

The lobby was a wide-open space. Its glass display cases reflected the bright track lighting and contrasted with the dark oak floor, assembled from original wood that had survived the fire, some planks scarred black.

Robert's eyes searched for a place to focus, a concierge, a sign reading "Start Here," but quickly discovered direction. Across the fire-scarred floor, the shirtwaist factory workers, the women and men, looked at Robert from a life-size print muralled on the back wall. The familiar faces, some dour and some seemingly hopeful, had gazed up at him from the book that had fallen open on his floor in the night.

"Haunting, isn't it?" came a voice beside Robert as he walked toward the mural.

Robert hadn't noticed the woman stepping in time with him, their paths converging, until she spoke. "Beth," according to her docent badge.

"Very," he said.

"Amazingly, that photo was taken the morning of the fire. From the clock in the background, we know it was just hours before the fire started. Exactly a hundred years ago tomorrow."

"Do you know who they are?" Robert realized his vagueness. "I mean—"

Apparently used to the question, Beth answered before he could clarify. "Some. Not all. We'd like to identify, to recognize, them all. But that is a painstaking process."

A process Robert knew well from his research at university, cataloging historical documents, seeking their origins and authors. "I understand."

With a gesture, Beth directed him toward a pedestal at the side of the mural. "You might be interested in the identity chart over here."

Under a sheet of plexiglass, a smaller copy of the photograph covered the angled top of the pedestal. This one with the details removed. The workers stood, and a few sat, in silhouette, each with a number printed where their face should be. The numbers were repeated in sequence on the panel to the right, some followed by a name and a few details, others simply by the word "unidentified."

Excited by the information, Robert scanned the list of names for the initials "MTZ," then scanned it again more carefully, stopping at every "M," every "T." There were no "Zs," except in the name Lazlo, identifying a Hungarian immigrant.

"You're looking for someone?" said Beth, her voice tending toward grave, full of interest.

"A ghost, I'm afraid." Robert's stare returned to the silhouettes, looking for one that matched the form in the window.

"I'll leave you to your search, but don't hesitate to ask questions." Beth gestured toward a narrow shelf next to the display stacked with books, copies of the one Robert had been reading. "The book is only nineteen-ninety-five, if you're interested." One copy showed the photo on the cover. Another was opened to the silhouette page.

Robert thanked Beth as she walked back to the front, kicking himself for falling asleep before finishing the book. When none of the silhouettes on the pedestal or faces on the wall looked familiar or beckoned to him, as he imagined, he toured the rest of the museum.

Standees of workers silently operated rescued machinery in one section and the glass cases displayed tools and instruments and personal items found in the debris. While looking through them, he and Beth talked casually about the museum and displays.

Having lost track of time, Robert worried about being late for his appointment at the library. Since the battery had died on his watch, he had been relying on his phone's clock. Standing next to Beth, he was more embarrassed to pull the antiquated model out of his pocket than to pretend he had none. "Do you have the time?" he asked her.

Beth looked high on the side wall. As Robert followed her gaze to the clock from the photo hanging there, he thought it was time to start looking somewhere other than at his shoes all the time.

"A local clockmaker and artist restored it," she said. "It's accurate and beautiful."

A portion of the big clock was missing, its silhouette restored with heavy wire. Sewing needle shaped hands glistened with reflected light. The minute hand was poised at the edge of the void in the silhouetted face and past when Robert needed to leave. "I'm sorry," he said. "I really must leave now, but I'll be back."

Robert rushed from the museum, hoping Beth didn't think he was just avoiding a book purchase, worrying about being late to the library, and feeling he was running out of time for something even more important.

Part 3: The Gift

Robert timed his emergence from the museum entrance into the flow of bodies on the sidewalk. His speed and direction were not entirely his to choose, but he was on the quickest route to the library and arrived on time for his meeting with Ms. Bernard.

Since the open position was with the city and "subject to a rigid pay scale," negotiations were mercifully simple. Ms. Bernard, Jane, explained the conditions and offered Robert the weekend to think about it, but he accepted and signed before leaving her office. It was too late to worry about seeming desperate.

Robert's only complaint was that the city needed a week to finalize his employment, print his badge, and authorize his network credentials. And though Jane appreciated his enthusiasm, if he visited the library before then, it would be as a patron. Yes, he could volunteer.

With the job search behind him, and his finances curving upward, Robert concentrated on only two things as he left the library: the antique shop on fourth and how long, at his new income level, he had to save to afford one of those museum lofts. The money didn't add up. Not without a roommate. Yeah, it didn't add up.

The antique shop was the more immediate concern anyway, and a bell rang over the door as he walked in. Robert hadn't been in the shop before, but had noticed the vintage hats and women's accessories displayed in the show window on his walks. He went straight to that section, prompting a "Looking for a Valentine's gift?" from the man behind the counter.

Valentine? It had been a long while since Robert had bothered with the significance of the day, but agreed he was. "I'm looking for one of those things women used to hold their hair up," he said.

"I have nicer hair combs here in the case," said the man. "Very nice."

"Not to comb her hair. To hold it."

"Still a comb. Come see," he said. "In the case."

As Robert approached, the man unlocked the case and Robert's eyes locked on an antique tortoiseshell comb trimmed in silver on the top shelf. It was beautiful and perfect and too expensive. Robert looked at the balance in his checkbook and offered what he could. The man just glared at him.

Pulling his coat sleeve above his watch, Robert asked, "Will you take the watch for the difference? Until I can buy it back."

"I'm an antique dealer, not a pawnshop."

Robert knew every antique dealer was also a pawnbroker, but didn't argue. "It's a classic. It was my father's." He took off the watch and set it on the case, noticing the man's eyes following the watch from wrist to counter. "It needs a battery," he said, as the man picked it up. "The band alone..." he started, but the man already had the watch under his loop.

"You have two weeks. Ten percent and the cost of a new battery."

"Three weeks?"

"OK. Three. No more. Plus battery installation charge."

"Deal."

"If she doesn't like the comb, you return it. But you still pay for the watch and a restocking fee." He pointed to a sign formally disclosing the return policy in magic marker on white cardboard.

Return it? How did the comb get here in the first place? Maybe she already did. In a roundabout way. Robert looked the comb over closely for any imperfection, any identifying initials.

"And can you engrave something on the comb?"

The man stared at him as if in shock. Robert didn't know if the problem was the late negotiation or engraving on the antique comb. Probably both.

"If you engrave it, I can't return it," Robert negotiated. "Just three little letters. Small as you can."

"What letters?"

"'MTZ.' They're her initials." *At least, I hope so.*

The man took the comb to his workbench. Robert pointed at a sign on the counter that read "Free Valentine card with purchase over $25. Heart bag with purchase over $50." "Can I pick out a card?" he asked, but didn't hear an answer over the whir of the engraver.

The man handed Robert the comb to inspect the initials, then took it from him and wrapped it in red and white tissue paper, still crumpled from its last use. He started to put the whole thing in a brown t-shirt bag when Robert pointed to the sign. He had spent over fifty dollars without the watch as part of the deal. The man reached beneath the counter and shook open a red, heart-shaped plastic bag.

The sun was setting by the time Robert got back to the apartment, but his gift could only be given after dark, anyway. He tested several pens on the sole of his shoe before remembering one he had accidentally pocketed at the library. In his neatest printing, he wrote on the card, "Thank you, MTZ. Your Valentine, RVP." Then he slipped the card and his hopes in the bag with the comb.

When the alley was dark, except the triangle of spilled streetlight on the far wall and the hint of moon rising over the rooftop, Robert raised the sash, checked that it wasn't going to fall, leaned out the window, and clipped the heart bag to the clothesline with two pins, and then a third. He pulled the return line slowly, watching the bag drift into the void. Gently pulling, pulley groaning, the bag reached the far wall.

The armchair still sat near the window, still needing reupholstered, so Robert sat and watched and waited.

When the moon was high overhead, the awning window glided out, catching the moon on the angled glass and illuminating the window. The glowing silhouette of a hand plucked the bag from the line, then the arm, the hand, and the bag disappeared through the open window that closed with the same "thunk" as the night before.

Robert was wondering if he would ever know what came of the comb when the window illuminated like his grandma's old tube TV screen, revealing a woman pinning her hair up, the glint of the silver-trimmed tortoiseshell sparkling in her hair. The window went dark as a cloud passed before the moon.

Robert was certain the show was over for the evening, but he could not rest. The book. His research skills were as rusty as the clothesline pulley. He opened the book and flipped to the back, looking for an index, and found a list of names—everyone known to work at the factory in the months leading up to the fire. Flipping to the end of the names sorted alphabetically by last name, he found his Valentine.

Zeller, Mary Theresa.

"Mary Theresa Zeller."

"MTZ"

In the morning, after one more inspection of the factory window across the alley, Robert walked to the museum. He hadn't noted the hours of operation the day before, so waited the twenty or so minutes, pacing the concrete alcove from the door to the sidewalk and back while people dressed for business walked past.

Robert was at the sidewalk end of his route when he heard the clunk of the door latch behind him. He turned to see a woman through the tinted glass, dark hair, dark clothes, silhouetted by the lights behind her. She pushed the door open as he approached. It was Beth, the docent. "Good morning," she said, holding the door for him.

"Good morning. I said I'd be back," he said, and then thought what a stupid thing to say.

"You didn't lie," she said.

She was just being kind. It's her job. "Thank you," he said, walking past her into the open space, across the scarred floor, and to the photo wall. This time, Beth went to the display cases instead of following him.

Starting at one end, Robert scanned the photo, sidestepping across the floor as he inspected the hairdos, searching for the comb. With the women facing forward, their hair ties in the back, Robert realized the flaw in his brilliant plan. There were other photos of the women taken at different angles. He could search them... But wouldn't have to. In less time than he had paced the concrete out front, he found his answer.

There, near the front, stood one of the few smiling women, her head turned slightly to the side, her hair neatly curled up and pinned with the comb. Had she posed to show off her new comb? Did she know he would look for her?

"Mary."

Robert's search was over, but his mission was not. Looking over his shoulder at Mary, he walked to the display cases, and as it had caught his eye in the antique shop, the comb called him from the top shelf of the personal items display.

"Beth?" he called to the docent, who was straightening brochures one case over. "May I call you Beth?"

"Yes…"

"Robert," he said, extending his hand as she approached. For the third time that week, that month, and as it was only mid-February, that year, Robert shook hands with someone. Though Ms. Jane Bernard counted for two of them. The closest he had come to shaking hands with the landlord was handing the screwdriver back and forth.

"I think I've made a discovery."

Behind her glasses, Beth's green eyes lit up. "Show me."

Turning his head toward the display case, Robert directed Beth's gaze there as well. He pointed at the silver-trimmed tortoiseshell hair comb on the top shelf. "See that comb?"

"Yes," she said. "How strange. I hadn't noticed it before." She pinched the marbled black and amber frames of her glasses between her thumb and finger as if to adjust them. "I love tortoiseshell."

"Can I show you something in the photo?" Eager to share his discovery, Robert started walking that way without waiting for her response.

Beth followed on his heels. "It isn't…"

Robert pointed at the picture, at the comb holding up the hair of Mary Theresa Zeller, who smiled at him through time. "I think that's the comb," he said, fighting the urge to say more, to yell to the ceiling, to the floors above, "I found you. Thank you, Miss Zeller."

"I think you're right," said Beth. She walked briskly toward the case, sorting through her keys as she did.

Robert followed, excited by his discovery and pleased Beth shared that excitement. They returned together and compared the comb in the photo to the one in Beth's gloved hand.

Robert's brain ached as he waited for Beth to discover the etched monogram. He dashed to the stack of books and opened one to the list of names in the back.

"We're looking for an MTZ," she said.

And Robert was holding up the book to show her, his finger pointing to the name at the bottom of the list.

Suspicious, but not sure of what, Beth asked, "She's who you were looking for, isn't she?"

"Yes."

"That's uncanny." Beth examined him through her tortoiseshell eyeglasses. "How did you know..."

"It's hard to explain..."

"Is this when you suggest we talk about it over dinner?"

"Uhhh." It obviously wasn't. Robert's shoes begged for attention, but he held his eyes on hers, very green behind the tortoiseshell frames.

"I'm sorry. I didn't mean..."

"If you'd like," said Robert. Then he decided he should start with honesty. "But it will have to wait. I just got a new job yesterday, and I don't get my first check for a few weeks." He also decided that mentioning he had spent the last of his savings on the tortoiseshell hair comb and engraving was a bit too honest. If there was such a thing.

"Then I will treat you. If you'd like."

"I'd like that."

Beth put the comb back in the case and called the curator about the discovery while Robert admired the photo wall. But as he met the gazes of the women, his excitement waned, his delight diminished. He opened the book to the page of numbered silhouettes and the list with so many unidentified. He looked from the page to the face of each and hadn't noticed Beth's approach, but she was beside him when he reached the bottom of the list.

"Haunting," he said. And his mind formed a new plan. "Can you show me the lofts upstairs?"

About Mending Time

As a portal ghost story, *Mending Time* is typical of the *Flashing Lights* series. But as the longest story in the series, it is more "cinematic" and features more mystery than humor. It also has one of the longest prompts.

Prompt

A person mends another person's shirt hanging on a shared clothesline strung between two apartments. The other person reciprocates and the two people form a relationship through their shared good will.

Inspiration

As I continued to imagine and develop the story, it became a mashup tribute to *Rear Window*, the Grimm fairy tale of the *Elves and the Shoemaker*, and the women who lost their lives in the Triangle Shirtwaist Factory fire (March 25, 1911) and other sweatshop catastrophes.

For *Mending Time*, as for many other *Flashing Lights* stories, I researched factual historical events for context, and contemporary literature for flavor. But the story is intentionally vague on historical fact and only mirrors those events—this is pure fiction, not a history lesson.

Mending Time is also a tribute to my grandmother, Mary Theresa (Zeller) Parker, who was widowed at the early age of 42. My grandfather, Robert Valentine Parker, was born on Valentine's day (1897) and tragically died on St. Patrick's Day (1944) while on duty as a Denver firefighter (though not in a fire). One of many jobs Grandma took to make ends meet, raising my father and aunt, was working in a cigar factory—her job assembling ammunition at the Rocky Mountain Arsenal expired with the end of the war. She told me a delightful story of how the women at the cigar factory wrote notes and slipped them into the cigar boxes to brighten the customer's day. Imagine the delight when the buyer opened the box and found a note saying something like, "My, you're handsome" or "Thinking of you," followed by the sender's initials.

Mending Time could have been told in fewer words, as I originally intended, but I hope the additional length contributes to a greater experience. The classic short stories of Bernard Malamud (known for *The Natural* and *The Magic Barrel*) and William Trevor influenced the style of my portrayal.

Easter Egg

The references to canasta are a tribute to my grandmother who taught me the game (and then regretted it) and to William Trevor, known for his story collection, *Cheating at Canasta*.

Bonus: Ten-Word Stories

KEEPING WITH THE TRADITION of stories with very low word counts, these stories do not have titles. That would be more words, which would be cheating. Very short stories usually require more imagination invested by the reader. The "About..." section after each story gives my working title for the story. So, you can decide if the story makes sense.

Since most people are not familiar with this story form, the "What I like about..." section gives commentary about my objectives in crafting the story. Like poetry, these short verses rely heavily on word cadence and sounds. If you aren't interested in story craft, then skip these commentaries.

If you enjoy these super short stories or are interested in the art form in general, look for my collection and commentary, *Ten-Word Stories... with Commentary*, which includes eighteen ten-word stories, six-word versions of some, and a discussion about the art form.

Ten-Word: 1

PG: Horror/Suspense

Click.
Can't see!
Shuffle?
Behind me...
Squish, scream!
...Not me.

About Whew!

This is my attempt at horror/suspense. I rarely write in this genre, but I have edited a crypt-load of horror RPG publications.

What I Like About Whew!

The repeated and progression of sounds (the hard "c," "s," and long "e") and progression of punctuation, combined with the short words and sentences, provide tension, then quick escalation. Finally, "not me" expresses a horror trope. A grisly murder just happened right behind me, but I don't wonder who got whacked. I'm just relieved it wasn't me.

Ten-Word: 2

G: Fantasy, Humorous, YA

Black smoke... Vile acid... Burnt flesh... *Ogre!?* "Ugh. Dragon burp."

About Occupational Hazard of a Dragon Rider

As the writer of a fantasy series that includes dragons, this one was compulsory. I couldn't resist making it humorous, too (according to me).

What I Like About Occupational Hazard of a Dragon Rider

I like the deductive process expressed by the protagonist in this one. And the punch line. As a lover of dogs, incidents like this are not infrequent.

Ten-Word: 3

G: Fantasy, Humorous

Gossip, rumors, clandestine plots, forbidden romances. The mute gargoyle muses.

About Eavesdropper

I love gargoyles and like to think about what one stationed over an important doorway for centuries might know and isn't telling. If gargoyles could talk...

What I Like About Eavesdropper

Although the title is not part of the official story, I love the pun. The repeated and echoing sounds give the story a satisfying flow ("gossip" - "gargoyle," "rumors" - "romances" - "muses").

The six-word version of this story may even be better because it has good cadence and more punch:

Sinister machinations, secret romances... Gargoyle gossip.

Easter Egg

I contributed a gargoyle NPC (nonplayer character) named Sinister to an RPG supplement called *Infamous Adversaries*. The gargoyle became hostile after his companion and gossip mate, Dexter, was destroyed. Sinister had unusual characteristics from his centuries of eavesdropping on the important events at the doorway beneath his perch.

Ten-Word: 4

PG: Fantasy

Sun-shadow stripes cross the cracked stone, mocking my broken body.

About Dungeon Daybreak

This one is not necessarily fantasy, but that was how it started in my brain, and knowing that helps form the image.

What I Like About Dungeon Daybreak

By now, you probably recognize how I use repeated sounds to collect sections of the story or run the story together. The progression of leading consonants (soft - hard - soft - hard) helps build the "stripes" imagery and tell this story. The image of dark and light stripes caused by the sun on the cracked floor are compared to the dark and light stripes of the prison uniform worn by the broken body collapsed on the floor.

Ten-Word: 5

PG: Science Fiction, Mainstream

Fresh baked bread...
"Pardon the off flavors... oven's a dumpster."

About Apocalypse Baker

This story was intended to be fantasy until I introduced the word "dumpster." Depending on your druthers, it could be post-apocalyptic or modern.

What I Like About Apocalypse Baker

I enjoyed turning the universal image, really aroma, of "fresh baked bread" on its head, while accepting the situation (people cooking over burning garbage) as not as uncommon as we would hope. The beginning and ending sounds of the baker's line create bookends, "pardon" and "dumpster," and the repeated "f" and "v" sounds through the middle give it a definite beginning, middle, and end. "Dumpster" makes a good punchline since it is a funny word itself.

Ten-Word: 6

G: Fantasy, Folk Tale

"Everything I do is noble. I am king... Hang them."

About Ignoble

This story invokes fantasy, but could be historical.

What I Like About Ignoble

This is comparable to "let them eat cake." Its terseness and concentration on self depicts the attitude of so many in powerful positions. Eight of the ten words describe the "I" as someone above others.

Secret Bonus: A Poem!?

I AM NOT A poet, which will become obvious when you read this short limerick-ish style poem. Though not short on humor, the collection was light on fantasy stories, so I've included this for your fantastical entertainment (and a bit of satirical social commentary).

The Dragon of Humbole

PG: Fantasy, Folktale, Poem

There once was a hamlet named Humbole,
Whose townsfolk did nothing but grumble.
"We have problems," they would say.
"A dragon eats our crops, then flies away."

"Bring us the King's knight,
"To kill that beast in flight,
"And end our troubles today."

But while the town lay waiting,
The dragon would come raiding.
"The problem is worse," they cried.
"The dragon breathes fire. Our homes are fried."

"Where is that brave knight,
"Who will save us from our plight?
"Before we have no place to hide."

And yet the people delayed,
By the dragon's ferocity, dismayed.
"We are finished. We are beaten.
"All our children have been eaten."

But there was no brave knight,
Only people filled with fright.
And that is what caused the town to crumble.

About The Dragon of Humbole

I wrote *The Dragon of Humbole* in 1995 in response to a frustration at work. Too many employees spent more time grousing about problems around the watercooler than trying to fix them. That never happens...

A note for those who are poets or study poetry: *The Dragon of Humbole* has the character of a limerick, but not the exact form. I expanded the fifth line into a triplet with an extended rhyming scheme across three limericks. I hope you enjoyed the form, if not the poem.

Final Words and More Flashing Lights

I TRULY HOPE YOU enjoyed this eclectic mix of stories and are eager for the next one. I realize not every story is for everyone, and I purposefully stretch genre boundaries, but hopefully you found plenty here to satisfy your appetite for speculative fiction.

If you did, look for more stories in the *Flashing Lights* series, including the time-travel novel *Replacement at Redux: Fleeting Moment* (2024) and other stories.

Flashing Lights: Short and Weird Volume 2 is mentioned throughout this collection. If it isn't available when you read this collection, it should be soon. I hope you can't wait for it and **subscribe to my newsletter** to get free releases of some stories included in that collection.

Thank you for reading, rating, reviewing, and returning for the next story. You are always welcome to contact me through my website at **johndparker.com**. Your feedback tells me what you want next.

About the Author

JOHN WAS BORN AND raised in Denver, Colorado, but has lived most of his adult life in a log home he and his wife Lori designed and built near the Colorado Gold Rush towns of Gilpin County. They split the warm months between home and a guest ranch in Wyoming, where John enjoys riding and training horses.

Over the years, John has written and edited many short stories and roleplaying adventures. He has also written and directed several interactive mysteries performed at historical sites and museums. Now, after a varied professional career, John dedicates his creative energy to writing, editing, narrating audiobooks, and designing games.

John models his fiction after the great writers of the mid-twentieth century who captured his imagination with their magnificent prose. Writers across the genre spectrum, like: Ray Bradbury and Ursula K. Le Guin; Dashiell Hammett, Agatha Christie, and later James Lee Burke; Louis L'Amour and Elmore Leonard, to name a few. Great stories become timeless in their telling. A tall order he seeks to satisfy in every story he shares with his readers.

John writes fiction in several genres and publishes under different pen names to avoid confusion for his readers and the Amazon AI. This separation is not to hide anything, but to ensure that when you search for his work, you find the genres you expect. So you don't find dragons when you're looking for cowpokes. (Though, that's a story John wants to write).

Each story he writes features some combination of one or more of the genres indicated below. You will find stories for young readers and adults in any genre and he will be clear if any story exceeds the equivalent of a PG-13 rating (those are very rare).

John writes **Fantasy and Science Fiction**, which often involves Mystery and Detective elements as **John D. Parker**.

John writes **Western, History, and Action/Adventure**, (also with Mystery and Detective thrown in) as **J.D. Parker**.

Finally, John highlights his work as a **game writer, editor, and designer** on **OpieGames.com**.

Index

Bookends and Miniseries

BOOKENDS AND MINISERIES ARE two flavors of connected stories in the *Flashing Lights* series. Bookends are shorter stories that are best (though not necessarily) read in order. Miniseries are longer stories that can be read standalone and in any order like most book series.

Bookends: Abduction Coordinator

Left: *Freak Magnet: Strange Attraction*, 37
   Right: *Eccentric Orbit: Fragile Cargo*, 103

Bookends: Age of Sail in Space

Left: *Souls at Sea: A Bermuda Training Voyage*, 47
   Right: *Derelict in Space: Suspicious Survey*, 125

Bookends: Rainbow Catch and Release

Left: *Rainbow Catcher: Capture the Moment*, 67

Right: *Rainbow Redux: Reflection Rescue* (see *Flashing Lights: Short and Weird Volume 2*, 2024)

Miniseries: Aliens in the Family

More excitement coming from Eugene Jones and friends.

Story 1: *Covered Dishes: Date with an Alien*, 6

Story 2: *Lonely Cannoli: Alien Italian* (see *Flashing Lights: Short and Weird Volume 2*, 2024)

Story 3: *Electric Blue Mocktini: Alien Lightweight* (see *Flashing Lights: Short and Weird Volume 2*, 2024)

Genre and "Gravity" Index

HERE, THE STORIES ARE categorized by subgenre and gravity (humorous vs serious).

Aliens

Stories that include aliens or the possibility of aliens.

Alien Factory: Rite of Ascension, 131

Covered Dishes: Date with an Alien, 6

Derelict in Space: Suspicious Survey, 125

Eccentric Orbit: Fragile Cargo, 103

Freak Magnet: Strange Attraction, 37

Souls at Sea: A Bermuda Training Voyage, 47

Fantasy

Stories with a primarily fantasy premise.

Dungeon Daybreak (Ten-Word: 4), 168

Eavesdropper (Ten-Word: 3), 166

Ignoble (Ten-Word: 6), 172

Occupational Hazzard of a Dragon Rider (Ten-Word: 2), 165

Folktale

Stories that include or are characteristic of a folktale.

The Dragon of Dalhart: A Dustbowl Tale, 31

The Dragon of Humbole (Secret Bonus), 174

Ignoble (Ten-Word: 6), 172

Ghost Story

Stories that include ghosts or the possibility of ghosts.

Dead Man's Hand: The Only Good Cheat is a Dead Cheat, 78

Derelict in Space: Suspicious Survey, 125

Full Disclosure: For Sale: Haunted House, 119

Hanky-Panky: Dirty Laundry, 25

Mending Time: A Line to the Past, 139

Shannon's Eleven: The Cold Get Hot, 54

Souls at Sea: A Bermuda Training Voyage, 47

Historical Fiction

Stories in a historical setting or include a strong historical element.

Dead Man's Hand: The Only Good Cheat is a Dead Cheat, 78

Mending Time: A Line to the Past, 139

Souls at Sea: A Bermuda Training Voyage, 47

The Dragon of Dalhart: A Dustbowl Tale, 31

Holiday/Seasonal

Stories that include a holiday or are typical of a holiday story.

Christmas Angel: Leaning Into Christmas (Christmas, maybe?), 61

Fall Colors: Death is Beautiful (Fall/Halloween), 83

Mending Time: A Line to the Past (Valentine's Day), 139

Horror/Suspense

Stories that are primarily in the horror/suspense genre.

Fall Colors: Death is Beautiful, 83

Whew! (Ten-Word: 1), 163

Humor/Humorous

Stories in the humor genre or are, according to me, primarily humorous.

Christmas Angel: Leaning Into Christmas, 61

Covered Dishes: Date with an Alien, 6

Dead Man's Hand: The Only Good Cheat is a Dead Cheat, 78

Derelict in Space: Suspicious Survey, 125

The Dragon of Humbole (Secret Bonus), 174

Eccentric Orbit: Fragile Cargo, 103

Fall Colors: Death is Beautiful, 83

Freak Magnet: Strange Attraction, 37

Full Disclosure: For Sale: Haunted House, 119

Occupational Hazzard of a Dragon Rider (Ten-Word: 2), 165

Shannon's Eleven: The Cold Get Hot, 54

Souls at Sea: A Bermuda Training Voyage, 47

You're Fired: Combustion Claim, 97

Literary/Character Story

For some, the "literary" tag is more frightening than "horror," but don't let this scare you. These stories are primarily "character stories." While the events of the story are important, the characters are central.

The Dragon of Dalhart: A Dustbowl Tale, 31

Mending Time: A Line to the Past, 139

Mainstream/Modern

Stories typical of mainstream fiction or are dependent on their modern setting.

Apocalypse Baker (Ten-Word: 5), 170

Christmas Angel: Leaning Into Christmas, 61

Covered Dishes: Date with an Alien, 6

Eccentric Orbit: Fragile Cargo, 103

Fall Colors: Death is Beautiful, 83

Full Disclosure: For Sale: Haunted House, 119

Hanky-Panky: Dirty Laundry, 25

Mending Time: A Line to the Past, 139

Rainbow Catcher: Capture the Moment, 67

Shannon's Eleven: The Cold Get Hot, 54

You're Fired: Combustion Claim, 97

Mystery

Stories in the mystery genre or have a mystery central to the story. Most of the stories include a "twist," but not significant enough to qualify for this tag.

Covered Dishes: Date with an Alien, 6
Fall Colors: Death is Beautiful, 83
Hanky-Panky: Dirty Laundry, 25
Mending Time: A Line to the Past, 139

Portal

Stories that include a mystical portal between places and/or times.

Mending Time: A Line to the Past, 139
Rainbow Catcher: Capture the Moment, 67

Satire

Stories where the humor is satire. Most of the stories are humorous, but don't qualify for this specific tag where using the characteristics of something to make fun of it is central to the story.

The Dragon of Humbole (Secret Bonus), 174
Fall Colors: Death is Beautiful, 83

Science Fiction

Stories soundly in the sci-fi genre.

Alien Factory: Rite of Ascension, 131
Apocalypse Baker (Ten-Word: 5), 170

Covered Dishes: Date with an Alien, 6

Derelict in Space: Suspicious Survey, 125

Eccentric Orbit: Fragile Cargo, 103

Freak Magnet: Strange Attraction, 37

Mending Time: A Line to the Past, 139

Rainbow Catcher: Capture the Moment, 67

Souls at Sea: A Bermuda Training Voyage, 47

You're Fired: Combustion Claim, 97

Serious

Stories that are intended to be considered seriously. They may still include humor, but it is not central to the story's theme.

Alien Factory: Rite of Ascension, 131

The Dragon of Dalhart: A Dustbowl Tale, 31

Western

Ayep. Westerns. Stories set in the frontier era of the American West or are primarily a western story. (*Outland*, the sci-fi movie is a western—*High Noon* in space—so don't be surprised to find a sci-fi title with this tag).

Covered Dishes: Date with an Alien (almost), 6

Dead Man's Hand: The Only Good Cheat is a Dead Cheat, 78

Young Adult (YA)

Stories that include young adult main characters or are especially relevant to tween to teen readers. A young adult tag doesn't mean the story is not suitable for adults.

Alien Factory: Rite of Ascension, 131

Christmas Angel: Leaning Into Christmas, 61

The Dragon of Dalhart: A Dustbowl Tale, 31

Occupational Hazzard of a Dragon Rider (Ten-Word: 2), 165

Rainbow Catcher: Capture the Moment, 67

Length Index

It might seem weird to categorize by length, but story length affects storytelling style. Approximate word counts are given with each story form.

Ten-Word Stories (you guessed it, 10 words)

Apocalypse Baker (Ten-Word: 5), 170

Dungeon Daybreak (Ten-Word: 4), 168

Eavesdropper (Ten-Word: 3), 166

Ignoble (Ten-Word: 6), 172

Occupational Hazzard of a Dragon Rider (Ten-Word: 2), 165

Whew! (Ten-Word: 1), 163

Flash Fiction (<~1000 words)

With so few words to tell a story, flash fiction often leaves more to the reader's imagination than longer short fiction.

Note to flash fiction fanatics: After editing for this collection, some of the flash fiction stories exceed the one thousand word limit, but who's counting?

Christmas Angel: Leaning Into Christmas, 61

Dead Man's Hand: The Only Good Cheat is a Dead Cheat, 78

Derelict in Space: Suspicious Survey, 125

Full Disclosure: For Sale: Haunted House, 119

Hanky-Panky: Dirty Laundry, 25

Shannon's Eleven: The Cold Get Hot, 54

Souls at Sea: A Bermuda Training Voyage, 47

The Dragon of Dalhart: A Dustbowl Tale, 31

You're Fired: Combustion Claim, 97

Short-Short Stories (~1000 to ~2500 words)

My distinction between short-short stories and (long) short stories is more about the type of story told than word count, but that distinction usually happens around 2500 words. (However, *Fall Colors*, which I have included in this list based on the storytelling style, is almost 3500 words).

Alien Factory: Rite of Ascension, 131

Fall Colors: Death is Beautiful, 83

Freak Magnet: Strange Attraction, 37

Rainbow Catcher: Capture the Moment, 67

(Long) Short Stories (>2500 words)

These longer stories read more like very short novels than the shorter forms.

Covered Dishes: Date with an Alien, 6

Eccentric Orbit: Fragile Cargo (when combined with *Freak Magnet*), 103

Mending Time: A Line to the Past, 139

Alphabetical Index

SINCE THE STORIES ARE not in alphabetical order, here's a convenient index to find a specific story by name.

Alien Factory: Rite of Ascension, 131

Apocalypse Baker (Ten-Word: 5), 170

Christmas Angel: Leaning Into Christmas, 61

Covered Dishes: Date with an Alien, 6

Dead Man's Hand: The Only Good Cheat is a Dead Cheat, 78

Derelict in Space: Suspicious Survey, 125

The Dragon of Dalhart: A Dustbowl Tale, 31

The Dragon of Humbole (Secret Bonus), 174

Dungeon Daybreak (Ten-Word: 4), 168

Eavesdropper (Ten-Word: 3), 166

Eccentric Orbit: Fragile Cargo, 103

Fall Colors: Death is Beautiful, 83

Freak Magnet: Strange Attraction, 37

Full Disclosure: For Sale: Haunted House, 119

Hanky-Panky: Dirty Laundry, 25

Ignoble (Ten-Word: 6), 172

Mending Time: A Line to the Past, 139

Occupational Hazzard of a Dragon Rider (Ten-Word: 2), 165

Rainbow Catcher: Capture the Moment, 67

Shannon's Eleven: The Cold Get Hot, 54

Souls at Sea: A Bermuda Training Voyage, 47

Whew! (Ten-Word: 1), 163

You're Fired: Combustion Claim, 97

Copyright of Included Works